Coincidental Cowgirl

By Jillian Neal

Coincidental Cowgirl
Written by Jillian Neal
Cover Design by The Killion Group, Inc.
Edited by Chasity Jenkins-Patrick

Published by Realm Press
36 South Court Square
Suite 300
Newnan GA 30263
http://realmpress.net/

ISBN 978-1-940174-28-0
Library of Congress Control Number: 2015951950

First Edition

First Printing – December 2015

Dear Friends,

Welcome to Pleasant Glen, Nebraska, home of Camden Ranch and all of the captivating characters that reside there. This book is a continuation of Brock and Hope's story from Gypsy Hope (Book #4 in the Gypsy Beach Series), but don't worry, you don't have to have read Gypsy Hope to enjoy Coincidental Cowgirl. You can head back to Gypsy Beach for the beginning of their story later, if you'd like.

Brock and Hope are now married and have recently moved to Camden Ranch so Brock can take over his portion of his family's lands. In this book, as in all of my books, I hope to affirm the most important things in life: love, family, community, forgiveness, and impassioned sexual experiences that bring about growth in a relationship. Brock and Hope quickly discover that the first few years of marriage can be tricky. It's a steep learning curve, to be certain. I sincerely hope you enjoy reading the next part of their journey.

Before I began this introduction to the Camden Ranch series, I spent many long hours chatting with a dear childhood friend of mine. It was so much fun to reconnect. This was one of my dearest friends all through school, and we don't get to talk nearly as often as we would like. She's solely responsible for my love of the romance genre, too. One day, many, many years ago, we were standing at her locker and she handed me a deliciously thick book with a picture on the cover that immediately had my attention. There was a lovely blonde woman dressed in a beautiful gown caught up in the arms of a dashingly handsome pirate. "Don't break the spine or my mom will know we read it," she whispered to me as she placed the prized possession in my adolescent hands. I loved to read. I read endlessly, but nothing had ever enthralled me quite like that novel. I probably read the book cover to cover four times that week alone. The title of the book, "The Magic," perfectly described how I felt about the story. I've been hooked on romance and love ever since.

Although my friend and I have laughed over that moment many times in the last 20+ years, that wasn't why I contacted her. She lived in Nebraska for many, many years in her adult life, and if I was going to set a series there, I wanted to know everything from just what exactly a Runza tastes like to how much snow they really get on any given day. I wanted every detail she could provide on life in Nebraskan ranch lands, even the seemingly insignificant. She talked and I took meticulous notes on every single thing she shared. I also dedicated Coincidental Cowgirl to her. I don't think I could have captured Nebraska on the pages of this book without her.

As the cover indicates, this book is but an introduction to this series. Several of the Camden cousins will have their own stories in 2016. I'm so thrilled to add Pleasant Glen to my repertoire of fictional locales. I live in a tiny town and though I occasionally lament the fact that the grocery store bagger knows entirely too much about my regular purchases, I do love small towns. I've tried to capture the sweet insanity that can come from living where everyone knows everything about everyone else.

As for the cattle, I have a little experience with that, as well. At the ripe old age of 10, I helped a mama cow birth her calf. A few years ago, I won a ribbon for milking a cow while accompanying my eldest son's class on a field trip to a dairy farm. No six-year-old can out milk me, I tell you. I've done a little horse back riding and still have the slight scar on my chest where a horse decided to take a nibble of me. Although I didn't know it at the time, all of my childhood experiences on my grandfather's farm would come to fruition in my writing some twenty years later. You never really know where life will take you. All we can do is hold on and enjoy the ride.

I do hope you love reading Coincidental Cowgirl as much as I enjoyed writing it. I cried several times. I laughed even more. I always try to capture the essence of real life in my novels. Life comes with a wide range of emotions, and if I did my job, you'll find them all tucked safely between the covers of this book.

Happy Reading!

Love,

To Kelli - my lifelong friend.
Explainer of all pre-teen things,
introducer of Aqua-Net,
giver of my first romance novel,
and (many years later)
my unofficial informant
on all things Nebraska.

"Sometimes you find yourself in the middle of nowhere, and sometimes in the middle of nowhere, you find yourself. "

-Author Unknown

Table Of Contents

Chapter One

Lonely and exhausted were two things Hope Camden was beginning to associate with winter in Nebraska. She stared at the dent, the approximate shape of her sexy husband Brock's head, on the pillow beside her. Tucking herself deeper under the sheets and electric blanket and squeezing her eyes shut tighter didn't help. Brock was causing the racket that had awoken her, trenching out their little prairie-ranch cottage with the tractor-driven snowplow. She fought not to groan. Bellowing cows and the grind of tractors had become her early morning alarm clock ever since they'd moved to his family's cattle ranch six weeks before. If only they had a snooze button.

Overtaken by another deep yawn, she shifted and felt the tender, rubbed sensation between her legs from the way Brock had taken her so thoroughly the night before. The reminder brought a slight grin to her features. Yeah, four months of marriage hadn't dampened their sexual appetite at all. Hope just wished he was there for more than late night sex sessions before he fell into an exhaustive sleep.

She'd gotten spoiled the first few months of their marriage. They'd lived in her rental house on Gypsy Beach, the town that had raised her. Memories of the warm shorelines had taken to taunting her as of late. Their extended honeymoon had not only afforded Brock the opportunity to heal from a nasty fall he'd taken off of a roof. It had allowed them to bask in one another constantly. She missed waking up in his arms, talking to him all day long about what their life might be, recalling memories from her childhood she'd lost along with her parents when she was only ten, and listening to him tell her all about life on his family's ranch. Somehow, his cowboy stories sounded far more glamorous than anything she'd yet experienced in Pleasant Glen. All of their talking would eventually led them to her bed. She'd been relatively inexperienced right up until she'd asked Brock to show her everything she'd been missing out on. In her twenty-six years of life, she'd never felt anything as astounding as being taken fully by her husband. The way he dominated her every sense and filled her with his unending love was perfect. Now they skipped the talking, the reminiscing, the dreaming, and just made time for the sex.

Sighing, she sat up in bed. The sun was barely up, not that the sunlight changed much hour to hour when the entire world was swallowed up in feet of snow. As soon as Brock made the path out of their home navigable, he'd head to the ponds all over Camden Ranch to bust through the ice so the horses and cattle would have water. Then he'd be off to run the feed trucks.

He'd announced the evening before that he was going to a bull sale that afternoon with his Uncle Ev and his cousins, Grant and Austin. He'd promised to be back in time for a late supper. Not that his promise necessarily meant anything. The night before, two sick calves had kept him in the barn until midnight. The evening before that, yet another flat tire on his truck had to be repaired, and then there was another round of feeding to help the cattle survive the harsh weather. Brock would never intentionally lie to her. Ranch life had just been rough as of late.

With Brock and his family working hard to keep the cattle alive through the winter, who was she to complain about rarely seeing her husband? The thing was she missed him constantly. He'd been her best friend for years. Now, she had no one to talk to. The lonliness was getting to her.

She just wasn't herself lately. She wasn't sure she'd been herself since they'd moved to Pleasant Glen. Drawing a deep breath, she ordered herself not to ask him to spend more time with her. She was perfectly capable of figuring out life on this ranch and coming up with a way for them to be together more.

His uncle had brought up the idea of Brock hiring hands to help with his portion of the ranch again at dinner the evening before. Brock didn't want to take money from the family accounts until he felt like he'd added to them. Paying hands was out of the question in his mind.

At one time, Hope had admired her husband's work ethic and his stubborn resolve never to let anything beat him. He'd been through so much the last few months, including learning to read. As soon as they'd set foot on Camden Ranch, he'd thrown himself into the work full-force. He was determined to make the ranch more profitable than it had ever been in the past. He wanted to prove his worth. Hope certainly understood that after all he'd been through. They could survive one winter with him doing most of the work, couldn't they?

Standing beside the bed, she moved towards the windows to see if perhaps she could spot her husband on the tractor nearby. She scanned the expansive, snow-covered fields. He was nowhere to be found, and the freezing cold air sneaking past the window frame made her shiver.

Returning to the bed, she begrudgingly folded the sheets, blankets, and quilts back in order. Did other cowboy's wives always get up and make the bed? She wasn't sure, but something told her they did, and then they had a yummy dinner waiting on their ranchers when all of the work was done. That's what Brock's Aunt Jessie always seemed to do. In fact, Brock and Hope ate dinner up at his aunt and uncle's farmhouse most every night. All of Brock's cousins ate up there as well. That was just the way things worked.

Considering, Hope wondered if she could make dinner for her and Brock that night, just the two of them. That would be nice. They could talk and reconnect. She didn't want to hurt Aunt Jessie's feelings, but Hope really missed cooking. They were newlyweds — surely no one would be upset if they wanted to spend a night alone together.

While she got ready for work, she debated what to cook. Staring down at her thighs as she pulled off the jogging pants she'd slept in, she sighed, "Maybe not beef." Afraid to check the ancient bathroom scale left in the cottage by a previous owner, she went ahead and estimated that she'd gained a good twenty pounds since she'd gotten married. In Gypsy Beach, she'd settled into married life and had been able to eat more since she and Brock combined their incomes. That was where the first ten pounds had come from, but the second half had been packed on in the last few weeks alone.

It seemed beef was the only thing anyone in Nebraska ever ate. It was all delicious, but she couldn't recall the last time she'd had a salad. Beef stroganoff, beef tips, hamburgers, brisket, stew, steak; the meals all centered around red meat, and the extra helpings were definitely making themselves known. *Well, you're living on a cattle ranch, so that seems fairly logical. Even the license plates on the trucks say, 'The Beef State.'* She jiggled her thighs with her hands to add to the effect.

Not that Brock would ever complain about her added weight. Oddly, he seemed very pleased with it. When they *were* alone, he couldn't keep his hands off of her rapidly thickening curves. She loved that, but all of her jeans were getting uncomfortably tight, and it was entirely too cold to wear anything loose fitting to work.

Raising her head, she stared into the dresser mirror and lectured herself sternly. "You're being a baby. Buck up. You're the one who insisted the two of you move up here, so make the best of it." She'd repeated that same speech to herself several times as of late. It was true. When they'd visited the ranch back in September, she'd been certain Pleasant Glen would make the perfect home for the two of them. Her Gypsy side had told her so. Of course, back then their *home* wasn't buried in multiple feet of snow and constantly freezing, and her Gypsy side seemed to be on hiatus as of late. She couldn't settle in. Her heritage was much easier to access in a beach town full of Gypsies. Here, she was going to have to work harder to locate herself, it seemed.

Shaking her head, she clenched her jaw in determination. She would not complain about the ranch to Brock. This was his family's land. He loved being there. Things would get better. He wouldn't always work endless hours. If nothing else, spring had to arrive eventually, didn't it? She'd be fine. She just had to get the hang of this cattle business. That was all.

Digging deep, she considered. A meal at home that didn't involve beef and spending hours cuddling and reconnecting would go a long way. She could do that. It wasn't Brock's job to fix her problems. She wanted to be able to save herself. Rancher's wives were a very capable lot.

Somewhat bolstered by her evening plans, she traipsed past stacks of boxes in the hallway they still hadn't unpacked. She'd been training to take over the library, and if it didn't involve a cow, Brock really didn't have time to deal with it. They'd get to that later, she supposed. Stepping around a large box in the kitchen, she grinned at the full pot of coffee he'd managed to perk for her before he left. As of late, the coffee produced from the ancient maker would leak out the bottom, leaving the carafe full of nothing but watery grounds. Brock had tried to work on it the afternoon before. It must have been a success. A full pot of coffee was even better than a love note, right?

You're married to the best guy on the planet, she reminded herself as she made a large mug of coffee and decided to scramble some eggs on the one burner on the stove that worked reliably. She melted a heap of butter in the old iron skillet and continued her regular morning pacifications. A new coffee maker could be purchased after the spring cattle sale, and maybe also a new stove. They could fix up the house when they'd made more money than she was bringing in from working at the library.

Their cottage house was lovely in the warmer weather, but currently it was twenty degrees outside, and the house didn't feel much warmer inside. Once again, Hope found herself wishing that her husband would lose a little of his stubborn streak and take his uncle's advice that he use money in the family accounts to at least fix up the house since he *was* working his ass off.

Putting all of that out of her mind, she sat down at their tiny kitchen table with her plate. Today would be a better day. She'd see to it. She'd go out in town during her lunch break. She hadn't really ventured outside the library too much yet. Maybe she'd meet a few people that hadn't yet stopped into the library to say, 'hi,' get groceries, and she'd make a fabulous dinner for her and her husband.

***

"Whoa there," Brock Camden pulled back on his horse, Cinder's, reins. The horse whinnied and shook his head as the snow flew back off of his Uncle Ev's horse's hooves. Tugging to the right side, Brock guided Cinder up beside his uncle instead of riding his flank.

"Every winter I think it's the worst I've seen yet. I been ranching since I was too small to saddle a pony, and I swear this one is the worst." Uncle Ev shook his head.

The icy wind bit at Brock's cheeks. It seemed to take up residence in the marrow of his bones until he was concerned they were going to shatter. The only time he felt warmth was when Hope was tucked safely in his arms, and that didn't happen nearly as often as he'd like, since ranching took up all of his time. He tried to remind himself that come July he'd be cursing the heat. "You got that right. I don't know how I'm gonna keep my herds alive 'til spring."

"Ah, they'll be fine. You, on the other hand, need to take it easy," Ev urged. "You need to hire some help or *you* may not make it 'til spring."

Had Brock's eyes not burned from the cold, he would have rolled them. He was growing weary of his uncle's advice. Didn't he understand that Brock needed to prove that he wasn't his father? Didn't he understand that he had to make money if he was really going to be able to take part ownership of Camden Ranch?

Many years before, Brock's drunkard father, Mick, had lost part of the ranch in a bet. Now it was up to Brock to show the whole town of Pleasant Glen that he was nothing like his dad. And he'd couldn't prove himself until he deposited a hefty paycheck into the Camden accounts from cattle sold in the spring.

Austin, Brock's cousin, rode up beside him. "Why don't you go take Hope to work? I'll go bust up the ponds. If you gonna be a stubborn ass and aren't gonna hire any hands this season, at least let us help you." He immediately joined his father's band. His customary smirk was frozen on his face.

"You sure you don't mind?" Brock deeply appreciated any help he could get, and taking help from his cousins was different than spending money out of the Camden accounts. They were family. They all owned part of the ranch.

"Nah, I don't mind. More work I do during the winter, the less Mom and Dad ride my ass about leaving in the spring and summer." Austin cut his eyes towards his father.

"We have never ridden your ass about anything, son. Your mama worries about you and your rodeo dreams. Can't say I blame her," Ev came right back.

"Yeah, yeah, I know. Mama'll be fine."

Brock shook his head. Austin's rodeo career was far from a dream. He already had several titles to his name, and he was well known on the circuit. Brock doubted he'd give it up any time soon. "If you don't mind doing the ponds, I'll go see my bride."

"Go on," Austin and Ev urged at the same moment.

Much to Hope's delight, Brock appeared just as she was dipping her plate in the soapy water she'd run in the sink. "Hey, you're here." Drying her hands quickly, she raced into his arms. Chuckling, he hugged her to his chest, but she couldn't access much of him. The hardened planes of his chest and his muscular arms that always made her feel safe were bundled up against the elements. The freezing cold was trapped inside his coat and chaps. It transferred to her as soon as she embraced him, but she didn't care. She'd endure the cold to be in his arms. There was nothing better.

He set his cowboy hat on the counter. The front hung off the edge, and Hope resisted the urge to scoot it back. Apparently, that damaged the rim and made cowboys unhappy. She'd deciphered that much in the last couple weeks. Maybe with a little more time, she'd figure out more about ranch life since Brock really didn't have time to teach her. She'd always been a quick learner. She'd figure out ranch life soon; she was determined.

Tugging off his deerskin gloves, Brock brushed a kiss on her cheek. The cold bristle of his slight beard stung her jaw. She shivered until he drew her back in his arms and mated their mouths in an unexpectedly passionate kiss. "God, I miss you." His hands squeezed her backside and just like every time before, she let her frustrations melt in the heat that emanated between them. "You okay, darlin'?" Concern darkened the golden rims of his eyes.

She angled her head, hungry for more, when he broke the kiss. Avoiding his question, she replied to the first comment, "I miss you, too." Her tongue stroked hers, coaxing her, tasting her mouth. A shiver that had nothing to do with the weather quaked through her body. Her soul longed to beg him to stay with her that day, but she refused to be a clingy, needy wife. The kiss provided a fantastic way to keep her from talking.

"I'm gonna take you to work. It's bad out there. Austin's gonna break up the ice on the ponds. We got another few inches of snow last night." Exhaustion had set in his soulful hazel eyes three weeks before. With every additional snowfall, it worsened.

"You don't have to do that. I'm sure I could get there on my own. I do eventually have to learn to drive in the snow, Brock." Contention perforated her tone. For some reason, her feelings were dangerously close to the surface that morning.

On her first attempt at driving in Nebraska, the rear tires had encountered ice; she'd panicked, and had very nearly driven Brock's new truck off in a ditch. Ever since then, he'd insisted on driving her everywhere. She added his overprotective nature to the list of things she generally loved but that were getting on her nerves lately.

"Nah, I don't mind. I like taking you."

"Okay, I know you don't but I'm feeling … a little … trapped … kind of. I need to know how to get around if this is going to be our home."

"Going to be?" His brow furrowed.

"You know what I mean. I need you to teach me to drive in this."

His eyes closed and he rubbed his hands over his face. "I will, sugar. I swear. I just love you so much, Hope. I can't stand to think about you getting out there and having an wreck. Nothing scares me. Nothing but the thought of something happening to you. Please just let me take you until I get a chance to really give you some lessons. Just give me a little time."

Hope's gut reaction was to be appreciative of his worrying about her, but he wasn't the one that had to be carted around. He'd been protecting her since they'd met in high school. It was one of the things she loved most about him, but at some point she had to *live* in their new town. "Thank you for worrying about me, but I can't go on never driving. Just promise you'll teach me soon, and that you really don't mind driving me to work."

He held up his right hand in a pledge. "Scout's honor, and when have I ever minded doing anything for you, darlin'?" His wink made her heart fly and the guilt in her stomach increase in magnitude. She had nothing to complain about. She had a loving husband, more food than she clearly should be eating, and a warm-ish house. He'd just promised to teach her to drive in the snow when he had more time. She just needed to be patient.

Refusing to nudge the thermostat up yet another degree before they left, she finished getting ready for work, added several additional layers of coats, scarves, and gloves, and then followed her husband out to his truck. Underneath all of that, no one could tell if she'd gained weight anyway.

Chapter Two

"Hey, I was thinking I'd make a nice dinner tonight when you get home … just for the two of us." She tried to sound nonchalant. Making dinner wasn't some kind of ratifying accomplishment after all.

"You sure, sugar? Aunt Jess is already up there cooking away."

"I really want to. I'll go by the Safeway at lunch. I want us to have a night all alone."

He glanced her way long enough to give her his sexy-as-sin grin. "I'm sure as hell not gonna turn you down. Evening at home, just the two of us, sounds like heaven, as long as I get to have you for dessert, Mrs. Canden." He winked at her before turning back to the dirt road ahead of them. "I miss you like crazy. I'm sorry I've been so busy lately. If we manage not to lose any stock through this, I swear it'll be a miracle." He gestured his head to the gray earth surrounding them. The snow on the sides of the road matched the leaden sky.

"It's okay. I know you're busy. Spring has to be here eventually, right?"

Grinning, he nodded. "Yeah, calvings better than busting ice and running feed trucks, for sure. I remember growing up here, thinking the snow was the greatest thing ever. 'Course, wasn't my job to keep all the cattle fed and cared for back then, and this winter beats anything I've ever seen."

"So, you mean this winter is worse than the ones here when you were a kid?" Good, maybe it wasn't just her that was concerned they'd accidentally moved to the Arctic Tundra instead of Nebraska.

"I don't really know. Probably not. You know how when you're a kid, you don't really realize what's at stake, so now it just *seems* worse than it was then."

Realizing what was at stake wasn't something she cared to think too much about, and she was an adult. One thing she had noticed, via the stories told around Aunt Jessie's dinner table, was that ranch work changed with the seasons but didn't ever really lessen. Holly, Brock's youngest cousin, who was working on her Masters degree at Nebraska-Lincoln, had assured her that autumn was the best time on the ranch in terms of cowboys being at home and not having to work so much, but, currently, fall felt decades away.

"Hey, Natalie's gonna pick you up for me. We're leaving for Laramie as soon as I get back."

Hope rolled her eyes. It was easier to pretend that Brock taking her to and from work at the library was a sweet, gallant gesture from a husband to a wife. When Natalie or Grant, two of his other cousins, had to pick her up, it was a glaring reminder that when it came to driving through snow and ice, she was completely inept. Being incapable was something Natalie liked to remind her of whenever she got the chance. Hope couldn't figure out why Natalie was such a bitch, but she preferred not to be around her.

The large truck bounced and rumbled off the five-mile dirt road that led from Camden Ranch to the town of Pleasant Glen. Hope gripped the armrest on the door to avoid colliding with the dash.

At least the paved streets had been salted and cleared. No snow was currently falling; that was something. The two streets, one either side of the railroad tracks, that made up Pleasant Glen were fairly easy to navigate. It was getting into town that was difficult.

Brock parked the truck near the library doors and gave her an extended good-bye kiss that left her short of breath and dizzy with need. "I love you so much, sugar. You sure you're okay?"

"I'm fine." She lied, and she was fairly certain he knew it. An evening at home alone with him would be all she needed. Lying to herself was becoming easier every time she insisted she was fine.

Keeping thoughts of them together that evening planted firmly in her head, she attempted to navigate her way inside the tiny library, avoiding icy spots on the pavement and towering snow drifts.

"Hi, Mrs. Camden," called from two passerbys as they headed towards Buck's, the new coffee shop on the corner that catered to cowboys and cowgirls.

"Oh, uh, hi." Hope waved. It was distinctly odd how everyone in town seemed to know her by name. She had no idea who these people were. Her Aunt Cora's castigating voice played in her head. *'Don't be shy, Hope. It's rude!'* It wasn't that she was shy, necessarily. It was just that she wasn't accustomed to everyone knowing who she was, whom she was married to, and where she lived. It felt a little intrusive.

With all of the might she could gather, she tugged the heavy library door open. All of the doors in Nebraska were weighted to keep the winds from blowing them open. Hope's body ached from the effort. The sense of exhaustion she'd had the last week increased its magnitude. Being cold all the time and being awoken long before sunrise was wearing her out. She needed more coffee.

She stepped inside the tiny Pleasant Glen library, her home away from ranch. The wonderful smell of books just waiting to be read settled the tense set of her muscles, but thoughts of *home* twisted uncomfortably in her stomach. Home, in her mind, was over a thousand miles away. In the pleasant North Carolina sunshine that warmed even the coldest winter skies. The place where she'd met and fallen in love with Brock. Where she'd helped him learn to read despite his dyslexia. Helped him make sense of the shame he'd shouldered over being passed through school for his athletic abilities. Their entire past existed on that beautiful shoreline. She admitted to herself that she missed it every single day. The place where they had time to talk endlessly, and he always seemed to manage to help her recall memories from her childhood she'd long forgotten. They'd been a team in Gypsy Beach.

She shivered and proceeded to unwrap the scarves she'd wound around her neck while staring out the window.

Her eyes landed on the Cut 'n Curl across the street, just down from the Methodist church. Hope contemplated. After removing her gloves, she ran her hand down her long, stringy blonde hair. She hadn't ventured to the Cut 'n Curl, and her stylist in Gypsy Beach hadn't been able to work her in before they moved. Her hair could definitely use a trim. She frowned at her inch-long split ends. Maybe she could stop in and see if someone could give her a quick cut and a blow-out for her evening at home with Brock that night. Her plan morphed from just dinner to an entire evening for the two of them.

Her mind conjured images of Brock's response if she happened to be standing inside their living room in the sexy lingerie she'd ordered two weeks ago. It was due in today. She'd been planning to wear it for Valentine's Day, but life was getting to her. Why not wear it that night?

Pink heat warmed her cheeks and genuine excitement bubbled in her stomach. Brock would love that, and so would she. He had mentioned wanting her for dessert. That sense of newlywed adventure had been missing the last few weeks.

In a moment of pure reckless abandon inspired by cabin fever, she'd gone online and ordered a beautiful purple and black lace bra and panty set. Due to her relative inexperience, it had taken her a minute to realize what open-panel panties were exactly, and that there were slight slits in the bra that would reveal her nipples. Trying to envision herself parading around in them for her husband brought renewed fever to her cheeks. She decided that she would to work up the courage to be wearing the lingerie set when Brock returned home from the bull sale, and she would stop in the Cut 'n Curl for a blow out. She definitely needed to start making some better memories in Nebraska, and she intended to start that night. They could have a great meal, fantastic conversation, and then have amazing sex. They could even reverse the order if they wanted. Whatever it took to get to spend hours in each other's arms reconnecting.

With a quick glance around the library, Hope wondered if anyone would stop in that day. She loved to help people find books that would entertain them during the long winter nights, but mostly she longed for the companionship. There was a time when being surrounded by books was all she needed. She used to run her own bookstore back at Gypsy Beach. Now, the bindings and crowded bookshelves seemed to mock her loneliness.

Heading to the back room, she tried to discern if she should feel guilty about having her lingerie order sent to the library. She didn't want one of Brock's cousins or his aunt and uncle stumbling upon it by accident. All of the mail for Camden Ranch arrived in one box at the end of the dirt road that attached the Ranch to town. Brock and Hope's mail made it to them eventually, usually via Uncle Ev. She certainly didn't want him delivering a box from Hanky-Panky Lingerie.

Hearing the front door heave open, she quickly returned to the circulation desk. A broad grin spread across her face when the woman that ran the Superette entered carrying a large box.

"Hi, Mrs. Winfield, let me help you with your box so you can look around."

"Oh, hello, dear. I'm not here for books. Miles," she paused to roll her eyes, "our illustrious mailman, delivered this to the Superette. I didn't open it. Miles must've. You know how the mail works around here." She set the box on the desk under Hope's nose.

A sinking sense of regret niggled up Hope's spine. Lately, she'd had several packages delivered open. She hadn't considered that when she'd made her lingerie purchase. Aunt Jessie had explained that Miles, the exuberant elderly mailman, couldn't read the addresses correctly and delivered mail to the wrong places, and that he often opened the boxes to make certain the items were intact before he made his deliveries. He considered it part of his job. Last week, Hope had received an open box of permanent hair solutions meant for the Cut 'n Curl and a large order of feed buckets intended for Merle's Feed and Seed.

She told herself that certainly these were all coincidences. Her lingerie would be delivered without incident. She was sure of it. Forcing another grin, she began unpacking the latest releases she'd ordered for the library. "Thanks for bringing these by, Mrs. Winfield." When she raised her head she noticed something odd. "Um, Mrs. Winfield, you have a few curlers still in your hair." Hope gestured to the two pink foam curlers still rolled tightly in the back of her hair.

"You'd think that idiot mailman of ours could figure out that we don't need a box of library books at the Superette." Mrs. Winfield rolled her eyes. "Here, can you take 'um out for me." She spun so Hope could remove the rollers for her.

"Oh, uh, okay, I guess." Hope nodded. "Hopefully, Miles will get everything figured out soon." She unclasped the curlers and handed them to Mrs. Winfield, trying not to think how very odd it was to be performing the task at hand.

"Thanks, and I doubt it. He's been the mailman for the last fifty years." With that Mrs. Winfield marched out of the library with a half-wave.

Somewhat disappointed that no one had come by the library that morning, at lunch time, Hope bundled up and headed out into the elements. She had a plan. Their evening alone was going to be perfect. Maybe she'd even confess that she was feeling a little out of sorts lately. Brock always helped her work through whatever might be bothering her. They just needed some time to talk.

Miraculously, the snow seemed to have finally taken a reprieve from unloading on Pleasant Glen with both barrels. There was still plenty gathered in high drifts against the shops and businesses, but the sun had broken through the clouds. A smile formed readily on her face as she dropped into Buck's to order a sandwich and coffee to go.

"Hi, Ms. Camden. Saw your husband headed out this morning. Must be going to the bull sale in Laramie. You know how many he's looking to buy? I've got a friend of a friend that might could get him a deal from a ranch that's headed to the auction block."

Hope's brow furrowed as she stepped out of the coffee shop cradling her lunch. She stared at the man in his early forties that she had never seen before in her life.

"Uh, hi. I'm sorry I don't know how many bulls Brock is purchasing." Not knowing that suddenly irritated her. Should he have told her that? The ranch work was another thing they didn't have time to discuss, she supposed. "Um, I'm sorry, I don't think we've met." She forced herself to extend the stranger her hand while simultaneously biting her tongue to keep from asking what business it was of his to keep up with Brock and his bulls.

"Oh, sorry, I'm Carson Rupp. I work at the bank in Kempton. It's the next little town after Pleasant Glen, between here and Lincoln. Sorry, didn't mean to come on too strong. I forget you outsiders need a chance to get used to everybody knowing who you are." He chuckled and shook her hand.

"It's fine." Hope didn't care for being called an outsider, but the man did seem kind. "It's nice to meet you."

"You, too; well, officially I suppose. Tell Brock Carson says hi. He'll remember me. I used to ref his little league games when I was a teenager."

"I'll tell him." Hope waved as she reached her first stop. Stepping inside the Cut n' Curl, her nose wrinkled as a cloud of hairspray made her cough.

"Well, hey there, Mrs. Camden, I'd just been saying to Sally I was wondering if you were gonna stop by anytime soon. I know we haven't officially met, honey, I'm Pearl." She extended her hand.

Hope shook Pearl's hand, but couldn't take her eyes off of the chairs in the old beauty parlor. There were two large poodles seated in both Pearl and Sally's styling chairs. The dogs were both draped in hot pink floral styling capes. Hope blinked rapidly, trying to somehow make sense of the image before her. She rubbed her eyes and futily hoped that perhaps what she thought were poodles were just two very unfortunate looking women. She had to be imagining this. She's seen human beings coming and going from the Cut 'n Curl. This wasn't a dog grooming shop, but when she focused again she was certain there were poodles sitting in styling capes having their hair … er … fur done.

"These are our dogs Miss Sue and Theodora. We're just giving them a little trim, and Miss Sue likes it when mama paints her nails and fixes her up pretty for her day, don't you, Miss Sue?" Sally proceeded to make kissy noises for one of the dogs.

"Uh …" Hope couldn't seem to verbalize any rational thought.

"Did you want to make an appointment, hun?" Pearl bustled closer and grabbed an appointment book off of what appeared to be an ancient console stereo from the 60's that she was using as a desk.

There was a Coke machine nearby from approximately the same decade. Vintage, harvest gold, hooded hair dryer chairs lined the walls opposite the styling chairs. Hope had read enough time-travel romances to wonder if the door to the Cut 'n Curl was some kind of portal to another time.

"It's Tuesday, so Sally's working the mortuary today. She's leaving here as soon as she finishes Theodora's deep conditioning treatment, but I could squeeze you in just before Mr. Henson's cock-a-poo," Pearl offered with a beaming grin.

"The morturary?" Hope squeaked.

"Yeah, poor Mrs. Davidson from over in Kempton needs her curls set for the great beyond. Her service is tomorrow."

Hope managed a nod. "Uh …" she glanced at the poodles once more and grasped the door handle to steady herself. "I can't. Well, I mean … I can't today. I just stumbled in … accidentally. Yes, that's it. Accidentally. Uh, have a nice day." With that she flew out the door. She'd let Brock cut her hair before Sally or Pearl came anywhere near her head with scissors.

What the hell? Maybe it wasn't her. Maybe the entire town *was* completely insane. *The entire town cannot be insane, Hope. Deep breath.* Visions of Brock's hysterical laughter when she told him that there were poodles in the beauty shop and that the stylists moonlighted at the mortuary soothed her shock somewhat. He'd grown up with Uncle Ev giving him buzz cuts on the ranch. He'd obviously never been in a beauty shop. She'd get Jessie and Holly to take her to their salon in Lincoln. Now she understood why they drove all that way for a haircut. There was no real harm done, and it would make for even better dinner conversation.

Determination stiffened her spine as she headed into the grocery store. She sighed when she discovered that the supply trucks hadn't made it through the storm yet. The produce selections consisted of squishy brown bananas and a sack of oranges. Her hopes for a salad withered along with the single head of iceberg lettuce she located. At least there were always potatoes. She grabbed a bag and moved on.

She picked up a few of Brock's favorite snacks and another loaf of bread, though there were three in the freezer. With every additional snow storm, she had to talk herself out of stocking up on bread and milk. Something about living in the South her entire life hadn't prepared her for existing in a place constantly covered in snow.

"Hey there, Mrs. Camden, how are you today? Saw Ev and Brock heading out of town on my way in. They going to the bull sale in Laramie?" Mr. Caruthers, the grocery store manager, offered her a kind smile.

Ignoring the slight irritation that clearly everyone knew where her husband was and what he was doing, Hope gave him a grin. "Yes, sir. They should be back tonight." Might as well give everyone full updates on his itinerary, she thought spitefully.

"Yeah, my son Brian just bought some property out near the McCovey's old place. He's bound and determined to keep buying land and keep adding to his herds. He went to the sale today, too. I'll tell you, ranch life is working him but good. He's struggling. I don't know how Brock and Ev keep as many head as they do. They're something else. I admire 'um. Salt of the earth, both of 'um. Ranch life is tough. I grew up on a corn farm. I told my daddy he was crazy to try and grow anything between the winter snow and the summer droughts, but we never missed a meal. It was a hard life, though, and now Brian wants to be a rancher. He grew up working my daddy's fields, so he knows what it's like to make a living outdoors here, but that's what he wants."

A genuine grin formed readily on Hope's features. Her previous irritation dissolved completely. It was tough. He was right. Clearly even people born and raised here struggled when they first got started. She shouldn't be so hard on herself or on Brock. Things would settle in just as she suspected. "It is hard. I've hardly see Brock since we moved. He's working so much. I'm sure it gets easier, though."

"I sure hope so. I'm trying to help Brian out when I can, along with running the store. I tell ya, I much prefer grocery marketing to cattle raising."

"Well, give Brian our best. It was nice to see you."

"You too, Mrs. Camden. I'm sorry the trucks didn't make it in. That was some storm. We'll have more in stock tomorrow or the next day."

"It's no problem. I'm just picking up a few odds and ends." Hope offered him a wave as she headed towards the refrigerator cases.

There was a paltry selection of chicken and turkey. She picked up one of the available whole chickens and tried to decide what to do with it. Brock wasn't a terribly picky eater, but he worked hard, was always hungry, and had been raised on a cattle ranch. He vastly preferred beef to chicken.

Before Hope's parents had been killed, she'd loved cooking in the kitchen with her mother. Forcing herself to feel the pain of missing her mom, she tried to recall anything they'd made with chicken. Chicken pot pie was an idea, or maybe soup. Roasted chicken! Yes. That was a perfectly respectable meal. She'd never cooked an entire chicken before, but it couldn't be that hard.

She picked up a few more staples and then strolled down the health and beauty items aisle. Glancing around uncomfortably, she noted three people eyeing her and her purchases. Didn't these people have anything better to do than wonder about what she was buying at the supermarket?

"Oh, Mrs. Camden, I've been meaning to get out to Camden Ranch to talk to you." A round woman with bright red hair and wind-pricked cheeks lunged at Hope.

Her apple red top and knit green hat gave her the appearance of an overly-rip tomato. "I wanted to get to you before Nora had a chance. I've decided we need to have a little chat about what kinds of books you'll be allowed to order for the library. Nora keeps going on and on about censorship or some other nonsense, but you and I both know that the devil is always looking through our keyholes. Sinful books in the hands of our citizens is just inviting him right on in for Sunday lunch with the preacher."

Unable to believe what she was hearing, Hope's mouth hung open stupidly until the woman finished her diatribe. She wasn't certain whom Nora was, but she liked her better than … "Um, I'm sorry, who are you again?"

A huffed gasp of offense blew in Hope's face. She fought not to cringe. "I'm Rhonda Bellamy. My great-great-great granddaddy founded this town. I'm president of the PTA at Pleasant Glen elementary. My daughter, Christina, played Mary in the Christmas play last year, and my son, Zed, came in fourth in the 4-H Ornamental Horticulture competition. I headed up the committee to try to keep that blasted cell tower from being built here in the Glen. If you ask me, cell phones are a passing fancy. Has no one considered the fact that people can see," Rhonda lowered her voice to a hissed whisper, "naughty pictures on the internet right on their phones? Satan's eye right in the keyhole. I'm telling you."

Dumbfounded, Hope squeezed her eyes shut for a long moment, hoping against hope that when she reopened them, Rhonda would be gone like some kind of deranged mirage in the desert. Much to her chagrin, Rhonda was still five inches from Hope's face when she blinked her eyes open.

"Okay, well, Mrs. Bellamy, the town gave me full purchasing power within the allotted budget for library books when they hired *me* as the librarian. I do try to order in requested items and to get books from every genre. I don't believe books should be banned or in censorship of any kind."

"Well, I think I'll just see if I can't speak with Brock about this, then."

Hope's brow furrowed in shock. She huffed her indignation. "And you believe that my husband will tell me what I am and what I am not allowed to have available in the library? Brock would never do that, and just for your information, the Camden family founded this town! So it was Brock's great-great-great grandfather that set up Pleasant Glen, not yours." Her face enflamed. She glanced around uncomfortably, unable to believe someone like Rhonda Bellamy even existed, much less that she'd attacked Hope in the market. People up and down the aisle looked on with a great deal of interest.

"I *believe*, Mrs. Camden, that it is women like you that Paul thought shouldn't be allowed to speak in church!" With that, Rhonda shoved her cart forward with her nose high in the air.

Shaken from the encounter, Hope's stomach twisted uncomfortably. *That ridiculous stupid woman! Don't let her get to you.* Between the poodles and Mrs. Bellamy, she was tempted to head back to the library and forget her dinner altogether.

Trying to summon resolve from the nearby shampoo bottle display, her eyes trailed over area where the condoms were shelved. She'd been on the pill for years. She was put on it as a teen to help with her irregular and horribly painful periods. There were no more refills available on her prescription, and she only had a few left.

The one other man she'd slept with before she and Brock had fallen in love had worn a condom. Hope hadn't cared for it. She also hadn't cared for the guy. Brock certainly wouldn't complain about her going off of the pill and switching to condoms, but she doubted that he would be overly thrilled, either. Besides, she loved the way he felt inside of her with nothing between them. Hope glanced back at Rhonda Bellamy, who was simpering near the toothpaste and glaring at her. As if she needed yet another reason not to purchase condoms, Rhonda seemed like the kind of woman that would share her opinion on Hope's purchase with most of the town.

Hope used what was left of her withering resolve to order herself to make an appointment at the town clinic and get the prescription refilled. *Maybe Dr. Moore will just refill the prescription and not feel the need to do an examination.* Dr. Moore was the one and only doctor in Pleasant Glen. There were certainly an endless number of other options in Lincoln, but that was almost two hours away. *You're a married woma,n and even if you weren't there is absolutely no shame in birth control.*

Dr. Moore had delivered Brock and all of his cousins. Certainly, he must write prescriptions for women often. It was just that Dr. Harrison, back in Gypsy Beach, was a woman. Hope preferred that. And then there was Mindy, Dr. Moore's niece, who served as his receptionist. According to Holly, Mindy held a very loose interpretation of HIPPA laws. She didn't see the need for discretion once she was outside of the clinic. *Who cares if someone finds out you're on the pill? It's the twenty-first century, for crying out loud.* When a cowboy bustled Hope out of his way to access the condoms, she made a quick getaway.

"You're Brock Camden's wife, aren't you?" A pinched-face woman glared haughtily at Hope as she unloaded her cart on the conveyer belt.

What now? Hope fought not to sigh audibly. "Uh, yes, ma'am." She attempted some semblance of a smile.

The woman turned to the cashier. "His daddy got run out of town by his own blood, and now his son's come back with some Beach Barbie like the girls right here in Pleasant Glen aren't good enough for the Camdens."

Hope accepted the sympathetic eye roll from the cashier. Brock's father was an abusive alcoholic that had indeed been run out by Ev and Brock's grandfather. That, coupled with the fact that Camden Ranch was the largest ranch in the county and they were the founding family, made the Camden's ripe for gossip. Hope had never in her life been referred to as a Barbie, however. She didn't even wear makeup most days, and she was barely 5'2. Leggy and well-endowed were not adjectives anyone would ever use to describe her. Did all of the town bitches shop on the same day or something? Hope made a mental note never to grocery on Tuesdays.

"And how is Sheila doing in reform school, Mrs. Zekeman?" The cashier offered a discreet wink to Hope.

When Mrs. Zekeman bustled out of the store with a haughty huff, Hope forced a smile. "Thanks for saying that to her. I'm not very good at comebacks."

"Ah, don't worry about it, honey, I swear to ya, only half the town is crazy. You'll settle in. I'm Kara Seeton. I live out on Seeton Ranch, my husband's family ranch. We're just a few miles the opposite direction of your place. Drop by anytime. We'll have coffee and chat. Brock and my husband were in riding club together in school. It'd be fun to get together."

"That sounds nice. Thank you. I'll mention it to Brock."

Kara's warm smile and caring concern helped a little to console Hope's irritated mood. Maybe she *would* get used to this town … eventually.

Chapter Three

"Hope doin' all right, son? She's been awful quiet at dinner the past few nights," Uncle Ev pressed as they barreled down the road heading towards the Wyoming line. Austin and Grant were in the truck behind them, pulling the trailer. Luke and Natalie had stayed behind to mend a fence and watch the herds.

Not really in the mood to discuss his wife with his uncle, Brock offered a shrug. "She keeps saying she is."

Nodding, Ev seemed to get the message. Brock was sure his uncle was also aware it was a lie.

"Sure as hell ain't any of my nevermind, but if your Aunt Jess or I can help her settle in, we want to."

Feeling his icy defensiveness begin to melt, Brock sighed. "I know, Uncle Ev. Thank you. She keeps insisting she's fine, but she's not okay. I just can't seem to get her to talk to me like she used to. She wants us to have dinner alone tonight. I'm gonna try then. I'm pretty sure she'd jump at the chance to go back to Gypsy Beach. This life is just different, and I'm the asshole she moved up here for." Defeat had set up shop in his gut a week before when he'd overheard Hope asking Holly if there was a season when ranchers were actually at home. She hadn't meant for him to hear her. That only made it worse. She needed him there, and he just had too much work to do to be around more.

In his customary quiet way, Ev offered Brock a sympathetic smile. "I'm sure she is homesick. No reason you can't take her back for a little while if you want. We can look after your herds for a few days, but I doubt that'll really help. She might not be talking 'cuz she ain't quite sure what she wants to say. Don't push her too hard. Just let her know you're there if she needs you. She'll come around."

Yeah, well, she seems miserable to me. How the hell long did you want me to wait? And I'm not there when she needs me because of this damn snow. "Yeah, I know."

"You done anything about the insulation or the heater in that cottage? I worry about you two freezing in that house. She's probably not feeling real at home if she's cold all the time."

"I'll get to it when we have the money, and I can get a little time. I just can't right now."

Brock didn't miss his uncle's discreet sigh. "You know, when we get the bulls back to the ranch we'll quarter 'um off. Let 'um have their own space 'til they're acclimated. Let 'um get settled in long before we turn 'um out with the heifers and cows."

Fed up with most everything and worried sick about Hope, Brock's temper flared. "Would you please stop comparing my wife to breed cows? What do you want me to do, stick her in a pen by herself 'til she's in a better mood? Or maybe we should break her like a fucking horse. Docile her right up 'til she stops being miserable and hating living here." He shook his head and stared out the window in disgust. There was no way to make this better. No one would buy off his large portion of the ranch and his stock in the middle of winter. They were stuck. They had a little savings left over, but not enough to get them a house back in North Carolina until they could both secure jobs again. Until the cattle were ready for sale, they were low on cash and high on stress. He'd really hoped that Hope would fall in love with the quirky little town of Pleasant Glen. He'd gotten it in his head that she'd want to go out with him in the mornings for feeding and hang out with him during the day.

He'd just never imagined that she'd keep the the library open every day, and he didn't have the heart to tell Hope that her job was actually costing them money. Her salary didn't come close to the gas and wear and tear on the trucks it took them to drive her into town most everyday. Not to mention the time it took to do it. Right now, the library was the only thing his wife smiled over anymore, and *she* thought the money she was making was buying their groceries and the few things she wanted. He sure as hell wouldn't ask her to quit. Wishing he could somehow be there with her more or make her want to be around him while he was working, he rubbed his temples and tried to come up with a way to make her smile again.

"Finally got something out of you. 'Bout damn time. Get angry, Brock. Cuss me out, yell, do whatever, but then do some'um to fix what's wrong. Hell, go beat the shit outta one of the trees, or Austin, God knows the boy needs some sense beat into him, but you bottling up whatever's going on and her walking around like there's glass under her feet that's about to shatter ain't doing nothing for nobody."

"I know that."

"Good. And I never meant to compare Hope to a cow, son. All I was sayin' is everyone, human or animal, needs to feel like they got a place to call their own, and they need some time to adjust. Somewhere they feel safe and *warm*. Where they can be themselves without judgment from anyone else. Where they can just relax. I'm not sure Hope feels that on the ranch yet. She might need all of our help to get there. 'Sted of being stubborn as an old mule, you might try to let us help where we can. We do have some experience living in this crazy-ass town in the middle of nowhere where the only thing that outnumbers the cows is inches of snow."

"I don't know what to do." Might as well admit that along with all of his other shortcomings, he was also a piss-poor husband. She didn't seem like she wanted to talk about it, and he hadn't had time to insist. Every time he tried to dive into the conversation, something else blew up in his face. Snow. Flat-tires. Sick calves. Downed fences. More snow. More feedings. It was unending.

"Your idea about talking to her tonight isn't a bad one. Just don't expect her to come around in one evening or one conversation. First year of marriage is tough. Be patient and listen to her even when she ain't talkin'. There's as many ways to right this as there are miles between our ranch and that beach."

"Yeah," Brock sighed. "I guess we'll see how far I get tonight."

Chapter Four

When she finished her shopping, Hope headed back to the library. While she was loading her groceries into the refrigerator in the back room, she heard the front door open. *Finally! Someone wants to check out a book.* She rushed back to the desk.

"Mrs. Camden! Thank goodness you're here. I have several packages for you." Miles the mailman loaded the desk up with several mailer envelopes and a small open box. His Coke-bottle glasses slid down his nose. He pushed them back in place and straightened his uniform. Her heart leapt to her throat. Her lingerie was probably right there in the box Miles had obviously opened.

"Oh, thank you, Miles." Hope braced as she glanced at the box, but breath returned to her lungs a moment later. There wasn't anything purple or lacey inside. There was a round of rope wound inside the box from the Orscheln Farm and Home store in Lincoln. "Um, I don't think this was supposed to come to the library." Checking the tag, she smiled. "This goes to Camden Ranch. I can take it for you when Natalie picks me up."

"You know, I checked that package myself. I didn't much know what you were planning on tying up here at the library, but I saw Camden on it. Must'a gotten confused."

"It's okay, Miles, but you know you're not supposed to open packages not addressed to you, right?"

Suddenly, Miles snapped to. He gave her a salute with his right hand. "Neither snow nor rain nor heat nor gloom of night stays these couriers from the swift completion of their appointed rounds."

"Uh, well, okay then." Hope found herself nodding confusedly. Her right hand rose from her side to salute Miles back before she realized what she was about to do. Good Lord, half this town *was* crazy and they were taking her right along with them. "There wasn't anything else addressed for the library was there? Maybe something you *accidentally* delivered to the wrong place?" Thoughts of her lingerie showing up at Merle's Feed and Seed made her queasy.

"I'll keep checking, but I do my best to get everyone their mail as soon as I can. Sometimes the stamping takes me a day or two."

"The stamping?"

"Yes ma'am. Everything that comes into Pleasant Glen Post Office serving zip code 69358-7004 has to be stamped per federal regulation."

A sense of impending doom as to the whereabouts of her lingerie purchase quickly welled in Hope's veins. She nodded. "Well, uh … thank you … for working … so hard … I guess."

Miles gave her another salute. "My pleasure, ma'am. For God and country."

Brock stared down at the information about the three bulls he was considering. He made out most of the words successfully but was struggling with fine print. Hating having to ask for help, he withered further. He'd faithfully attended the Davis classes for dyslexia back at Gypsy Beach. Hope had helped him methodically work through the lessons to teach him to read, but he still struggled. *Stop throwing yourself a fucking pity party and ask Grant what it says.*

For the hundredth time that day alone, he wished Hope was with him. God, he missed her like crazy. Whenever he needed help reading anything, she never made him feel stupid. She just helped. Usually, he didn't even have to ask. She always seemed to know when his dyslexia made something impossible to understand. He always wanted her with him. If he were being perfectly honest with himself, he'd have to admit that he'd let his

31

cock takeover far too often when he *was* with her, though. Being with her was the only time he ever felt complete. She was everything. The way her body bowed back for him when she begged for him drove him wild. Her tight little pussy swollen pink and trembling against his sheer size. The taste of her juices, the way her breasts swayed to the rhythm of his cock as he made them one, that sweet gasp of need she always gave him on his first thrust made saliva flood his mouth. Being with her was a pleasure he'd never deserve.

But he had to stop pretending that sex would make her happy again. If that were going to work, surely it would've happened by now. They had to talk, but keeping his hands off of her was next to impossible. She was a drug he never wanted to quit. The shame he'd endured his entire life disappeared in the heady mix of their cum. Her love healed every blow he'd ever had to endure. When they were in bed together, she seemed happy and fulfilled. That was always his goal. He just needed to figure out how to keep her that way while he was out in the fields, and she was in that damn library day in and day out.

"They look good. That one in the back'll make all the others jealous." Grant joined him at the pen, laughing. Shaking himself, Brock blinked away the fantasies that so readily painted themselves in his mind. He swallowed down raw regret and remembered what he'd come to the sale to do. He was going to make Camden ranch more profitable than it had ever been before.

"Yeah, well, there's no other animal on the planet with a higher degree of job satisfaction than a bull." Brock joined his cousin's laughter, though he felt nothing jovial at the moment. *You've got a job to do, Camden. Focus. It's all on you.*

"Ain't that the damned truth." Grant grinned.

"I've got several heifers coming on early. They'll be ready to sire sooner than later." He made one more attempt at the tiny print at the bottom of the stat paper attached to the pen. It was hopeless. "Hey, what does that say?" Choking on his own pride, he pointed to the paperwork.

"Oh, yeah, let me see that. Sorry, I should'a offered, man."

Brock bit his tongue to keep from informing his cousin that he should be able to read.

"You already know all of this. They're charging a shit-ton more for the one with an overloaded sac. You gotta load 'um yourself and all that."

Nodding, Brock scanned the ranchers until he located the owner of the bulls and headed his direction.

"Mr. Snyder, sir? Brock Camden." Brock offered Snyder his hand.

Snyder narrowed his eyes. "You Mick Camden's boy? You ain't one a Ev's."

What small portion of Brock's heart that remained intact after worrying over Hope for weeks sank rapidly to his feet. "Yeah," he made no effort to hide his eye roll. "Mick's my old man."

An irritated grunt from Snyder let Brock know he was probably in for it. "Nice'a Ev to take you back in after what your daddy did."

Irritation fed the ire already coursing through his veins. "I'm not my old man, never have been, never will be."

"Oh yeah? That remains to be seen, don't it?"

Brock refused to answer. "I'm interested in three bulls you got in the pen back there. We doing business or not?"

"Made the mistake of doing business with Mick once or twice. I'm still several thousand short. Don't suppose you're interested in paying his bills now are ya?"

"No, sir, I'm not. Like I said, I'm not my old man. You got an issue with Mick, you take it up with him."

"I'll sell ya the bulls long as the total includes the two thousand your daddy still owes me."

"I'm not paying my father's debts." Feeling his biceps flex of their own accord, Brock clenched his fists, ordered himself not to sink them in Snyder's smug face, and walked away.

Chapter Five

At 3:00, Hope scanned the road in front of the library again, looking for either Miles with her lingerie or Natalie to take her back home. She needed to get the chicken in the oven if she was going to have time to roast it and get everything ready for dinner before Brock got back from the bull sale.

Irritation tensed her jaw. Brock had promised to teach her to drive soon. That would make life infinitely easier. Her patience was just running a little thin after her encounters with well-groomed poodles and the grocery store bitches.

Before Hope could let her annoyance take firm hold, Natalie burst through the door. "You ready? We had a fence come down under the weight of the snow. Mama and I had to get it fixed since Luke's looking after one of the horses that's acting weird. I need to get back."

Hope narrowed her eyes but refused to take her day out on Natalie, even if her need for everyone to think she was important was rude and annoying. "I'm sorry you had to pick me up. I can drive in this. How else am I going to learn if I never get the chance?"

"I'm glad to see you show some spunk, *finally*. Family's afraid you'll end up freezing in a ditch somewhere. Brock's got enough to worry about without having to cart you around, too."

Brock's got enough to worry about. The statement branded itself into Hope's skull. She picked up the groceries from the back room and followed Natalie out to Aunt Jessie's Suburban.

She tried to watch how Natalie handled the SUV. It didn't seem terribly difficult until they got to the narrow dirt road that led to the ranch. That took some skill. Hope tried to remember her driver's ed classes in high school. All she remembered was Coach Meyers shouting at her because she'd been terrified to merge onto the interstate and had stopped on the on-ramp.

You're not 16 anymore. Get over yourself. Determined to learn to take care of herself without anyone's help, Hope went on with her plan. "Can I ask you something?"

"Sure."

"I need to see Dr. Moore, just for a check-up, nothing's wrong. How do I get there exactly?"

"Mama's got a bunch of prescriptions and stuff saved up at the house. She might could save you a trip."

"I need a prescription refilled." Hope offered no other information.

"Oh, well, Doc's office is about a mile past that little parcel of land that the McElroy's bought from the Henson's when they moved to Lincoln last year. You just stay on the main drag, and you'll see it. Normally, you don't need an appointment or anything. Just show up."

"Okay, I might do that tomorrow after work. I can get myself to town though. It's no trouble."

Natalie made no effort to hide her eye roll. "You might have to. Just take it easy. They aren't calling for any more snow 'til Sunday. Shouldn't be too bad. I'm going to help out at the shelter. Brock'll be busy with the new bulls. Holly's due in tomorrow afternoon. She's spending the weekend at home. You could wait on her."

"No, that's not necessary. I'll be fine. Just needed directions. So, if I stay on the main drag, will I see the doctor's office first or the land you were talking about?"

"Both. One then the other." The gleam in Natalie's eyes said she was being purposefully difficult.

"Thanks." Hope clenched her jaw. She'd locate it herself.

A smile readily replaced her frown when her cell phone rang from her purse. "Hey." She tried not to sound sappy in front of Natalie, but was thrilled Brock was calling.

"Hey, sweetie. We got held up loading the bulls, but we're on our way now. I'll have to get 'um penned when we get back, but then I'll be in. I promise. I'll be there for our dinner."

"It's okay. We're just turning off for the ranch now. I'll start cooking, but it'll take everything a while."

"Uh … maybe we could talk while it's cooking. I miss you. I love you so much, darlin'. Something doesn't seem quite right lately."

Her heart tripped over the next several beats. He'd just said he loved and missed her in the presence of his uncle or his cousins. She beamed, but didn't want him to worry about her. "I love you, too. I can't wait to see you. I'm fine, really." Glancing uncomfortably at Natalie, she lowered her voice as an idea sprang to her mind. Maybe they could extend the night she had planned. "Maybe we could spend the day together tomorrow. I think it would be okay if I didn't open the library for one day. I really miss you, too." *It's not like anyone ever comes into the library, anyway. We could make the night last into tomorrow, just like we used to in Gyspy Beach.*

A moment's hopefulness immediately drowned in Brock's regret-filled huff of breath. "I'll try my damnedest, okay? Let me get the bulls set and chores done tomorrow morning. Then we'll see."

"Okay, that sounds good."

"I'll see you in a little while. I love you."

"Love you too. Bye." Hope ended the call, grinning. If it didn't snow anymore, maybe his morning chores wouldn't take too long, then they could spend the day together.

"You shouldn't ask him to do stuff like that." Natalie's harsh tone shattered through the momentary optimism and contentment Brock's call had afforded her.

"What?" Irked that Natalie was listening in to her conversation, Hope bit her lip to keep from saying more.

"Asking him to take the day off means more work for all of us. Ranching isn't a 9 to 5, with two-weeks vacation, Hope. Not sure why you haven't figured that out yet. You don't live on a beach anymore. Brock's trying to support you, and you aren't really helping."

"What is that supposed to mean?" Hope clenched her jaw until her molars began to ache and willed the Suburban to move faster.

"It means that these are living breathing animals, and all of our existence depends on them. They aren't books in your bookstore. If you decide not to open up the store one day, animals don't die. Brock can't just up and decide not to feed his herds. Life out here isn't for the weak."

Tears stung Hope's eyes, but she refused to cry in front of Natalie. She also refused to speak to her anymore. She should have known better than to have asked Brock that in front of Natalie. Why hadn't she just kept her mouth shut?

Hope made a break for the cottage as soon as she was dropped off. She halted suddenly when she encountered a wayward cow blocking the path to the door.

Swallowing down fear, she took two steps backwards. "You're supposed to be out in the fields."

The cow stared at her, unimpressed.

The fence. A fence had come down in the weight of the snow. The cow must've gotten out. *You live on a cattle ranch, Hope. There are going to be cows.* She knew this. She just hadn't quite learned how to deal with them yet. Summoning courage, she edged towards the huge animal, intent on walking around her and making it to the front door, but in that moment the cow bellowed and headed Hope's way.

Panic surged through her veins. Her right foot slipped on a patch of icy dirt, and a yelp made it out of her mouth as she tried to steady herself. With one additional step, she slipped and landed hard on her backside. Pain ricocheted through her hips and embarrassment drove the hot tears out of her eyes. She'd instinctively tried to catch herself, and now her wrists ached and her gloves were soaked. A half-second later, she realized it wasn't ice-covered dirt she was sitting in, it was ice-covered manure. She fought not to vomit. The cow looked on, unamused.

The groceries had tumbled out of the sacks she was carrying, and the chicken had careened into a small pile of snow nearby. Momentarily debating sitting there and having a good cry, she suddenly recalled a scene from that old Christmas movie where the kid stuck his tongue to the flagpole. Visions of Natalie laughing haughtily while she pried Hope's hip out of a pile of half-frozen cow shit had her deciding to get up before the snow melted completely through her jeans.

Carefully, she got to her hands and knees, swallowing down bile as she stared into a pile of manure. She managed to stand, rescued the wayward chicken, and slammed the door once she made it inside the house.

Fury shot through her veins. Natalie and her bitchiness, Mrs. Bellamy and her insanity, Miles the inept mailman, the poodle-grooming beauty shop. It was just all too much.

Kicking off her boots, she peeled the jeans down her legs, convulsing from the smell. Favoring her left side to keep weight off her right hip, she marched to the kitchen, located a garbage bag, flung the jeans in the bag and tried to tie it. With her anger driving her, she ripped the ties out of the bag. "Ugh!" Like a woman possessed she wadded up the jeans and the first garbage bag, threw them in a second bag and tied it with slightly less vigor. She actually opened the door to the carport to hurl the bag into the garbage cans when she suddenly realized that she'd been about to go outside without pants on. She had to get it together.

Dropping the garbage bags on the carport, she slammed the door and squeezed her eyes shut to keep from crying tears of absolute frustration.

The icy water that had seeped through the denim had left her right hip raw. She couldn't quite determine if her hip was red because she'd removed a layer of skin or if it was going to turn into a nasty bruise. Seeing the shower as her only means of escape, she quickly headed to the bathroom.

Her stomach continued to churn from the entire experience. She ran a washcloth under cool water and wiped it across her face, willing her lunch to stay put. Her body swayed, and she gripped the counter, wondering what on earth would happen next. Exhaustion seemed to greet her as soon as she stepped inside their freezing cold house. She felt like hell. She just wanted Brock.

Stepping into the shower, she tried to gather herself as she scrubbed away her insane day. She reminded herself of the nice normal people she'd met, but eventually she gave in. Salty tears mixed readily with the shower water circling the drain. Her stomach continued to churn.

When she was clean, she did feel somewhat restored, so she pressed onward. She dried off, and lifted one of Brock's favorite Cornhusker sweatshirts from the drawer. Holding it to her face, she inhaled deeply, still trying to rid her mind of the memory of the smell of cow manure. Nothing smelled better than her husband's natural scent. It clung to the sweatshirt and further restored her. She pulled it over her head and gave herself a moment to revel in the feeling of being near him. After she pulled on some yoga pants and wool socks, she headed to the kitchen to make a pot of coffee. Surely, that would give her some energy and help her forget this ridiculous day. Ignoring the constant roiling nausea in her stomach, she turned on the coffee maker.

Remembering that she'd left garbage bags containing her jeans on the carport floor, she went to throw the bags in the metal cans now that she was fully clothed.

Her entire body jerked in shock when she stepped out onto the concrete floor with only socks on her feet.

Dammit! She raced back inside and slipped into her boots before completing the task.

When she returned to the kitchen, she found coffee cascading over the counters and dribbling down the cabinets below.

"Why can't I just have coffee? Is that asking too much! Ugh! You stupid, stupid, thing!" she shouted furiously as she grabbed towels and mopped up the mess, aware that she sounded insane screaming at a coffee maker.

Pulling the plug, Hope debated throwing the damn thing out into the yard, grabbing Brock's pistol from the hall closet, and shooting it. Envisioning herself trying to explain to her husband and his uncle why she'd shot a coffee maker helped her simmer down, though she suspected everyone would give her a pass, considering the insanity she'd endured that day.

Her blood spiked with the injustice of it all. Still determined to go on with her evening plans, she located her cell phone and looked up recipes for roasted chicken on Pinterest. They didn't have all of the ingredients, so she combined a few different recipes, hoped it would be half-decent, and slid the chicken into the oven. Next, she washed a few of the potatoes, wrapped them in foil, and placed them in the oven beside the chicken, only to discover that the oven wasn't heating.

"Ugh! Just work!" She slammed the oven door and then kicked it for good measure. To her shock, she heard the heating element spring back to life, but now her hip hurt even worse. Her temper wasn't helping anything.

She was freezing, and exhaustion weighted her limbs. It would still be a couple of hours before Brock made it back to the ranch. She set the timer on the oven, limped to the closet, and located a few blankets before settling on the couch.

She stared dejectedly around the house that still felt nothing like the home she'd envisioned back in the fall when she'd asked Brock if they could move into the cottage. She flipped on the television, but a solid layer of snow had covered the satellite weeks before, and they got little to no reception. *Of course.* Unless she wanted to watch digital snow on the screen instead of the real stuff out the windows, TV was not an option. Brock had offered to climb up on the roof and clean the dish, but Hope couldn't bear the thought of him slipping and falling off yet another roof, even if he had been a roofer for years and had only fallen because of another man's mistake. Fear had consumed her anyway, and she'd ordered him to stay on the ground. At that moment, she regretted her order.

A shiver worked through her weary body, and the fierce ache in her right hip wouldn't give her peace. Natalie's chastising words replayed constantly in her head along with being called a *Beach Barbie*, Mrs. Bellamy's demands, and the fact that she still had no idea where the lingerie she'd ordered actually was. This entire place was more than she could take.

Nudging the thermostat up another degree, she covered herself in all of the blankets and tucked herself on the couch.

Chapter Six

Exhausted, Brock eased inside the kitchen just after eight. *Oh, hell.* Gripping his forearm to keep from bleeding on the linoleum, he frantically turned off the oven. It wasn't smoking yet, but it was well on its way. Grabbing a dish towel, he wrapped it around the bull-inflicted gash he'd endured trying to pen the damn things. His gaze landed on Hope, sound asleep on the couch. His sweet baby. He just didn't know how to take care of her.

Stubbornly refusing defeat, he considered as he located several bandages in the cabinets that still largely held previous owner's belongings and doctored his arm. Maybe he did know how to take care of her. He'd been her best friend for fourteen fucking years. Lately, he'd been so consumed with the ranch and trying to prove to the entire state that he wasn't his old man he'd put his marriage on the back-burner. That needed to stop.

Whatever was in that oven was certainly no longer edible. Hope was a great cook, normally. Life was clearly more than she could take lately. Concern that perhaps she was coming down with something took precedence over locating them food. Easing to her side, he adjusted the blankets she was wrapped in and felt her forehead. She didn't stir, but also didn't seem to have a fever. Brushing a tender kiss on her cheek, he pulled his coat back on and headed up to Ev and Jessie's. He had a plan.

When he returned, a genuine smile had formed on his face. He could make this better. He could do right by her just like he'd always intended. Cringing at what appeared to have been foil wrapped potatoes at one time, he threw them out. The chicken wasn't burned through, but was probably so dry it would be like eating dust, so he tossed it as well. Placing the frozen pizzas he'd graciously been gifted from his Aunt Jessie's large drop-freezer on pans, he turned the oven back on and thanked the good Lord that the kitchen no longer smelled like burnt potatoes. After taking a quick shower, he changed into clean jeans and a thermal shirt. He had to do something about the heat in their house. The insulation needed to be redone, but that meant redoing a shit-ton of sheetrock, and it wasn't a project he could take on anytime soon.

Slipping back to the sofa, he dropped to his knees and proceeded to kiss his wife awake. Her eyes blinked open hesitantly and then goggled. "The chicken!" She shot upwards, but Brock gently kept her seated.

"It's fine. I've got everything taken care of. Just relax, sugar. You're worn out."

"Why didn't the timer go off?" She was still frantic.

"Probably because that oven is shit. Don't worry about it. We're having pizza. We'll still have our night alone, okay?"

"But I was gonna make you dinner, and I was going to be wearing something sexy when you got home."

The disappointment in her tone made his heart swell, unable to contain the sheer amount of love it held for her. God knew he'd never deserve her. "I think you're sexy as hell no matter what you're wearing. Honestly, I really prefer you in nothing at all, but you in one of my Huskers sweatshirts is about the sexiest thing you could possibly wear. Can I get in there with you?" He gestured to the cocoon of blankets she was settled in.

Her beautiful grin replaced the frustration that had set in her eyes in the last few weeks. She gave him a timid nod.

Chuckling, he climbed behind her on the couch. His heart ached. He just wasn't sure he know how to make her happy again, but he sure as hell would try. "I dug Sweet Home Alabama out of the boxes upstairs that we still haven't unpacked. Soon as the pizzas done, I'll turn it on."

She turned gently and buried her face in his chest. "I'm so glad you're here, and I'm so sorry about dinner."

44

"You have nothing to apologize for. I'm so sorry the last few weeks have been hell. I'll try to be here more. I know I've let you down."

"Brock, you haven't. I just kind of have to get used to living here." She shrugged and abruptly stopped talking. Yeah, they'd had the beginning of this conversation a dozen times now. It was time to go deeper, much deeper. Tears were probably going to be involved. He hated to see her cry. My God she was too sweet and too good to ever cry, but it was inevitable. He knew. Drawing a deep breath, he reveled in the perfume of Hope fresh from a shower, like the dew on spring flowers mixed with watermelon candy with a hint of her own sexy spice, the side she only ever showed to him.

Trying to come up with an opening more eloquent than, 'so it really seems like you hate it here, and I don't have a way to fix it', he considered for a moment.

"I'm sorry I asked you to stay with me tomorrow. I shouldn't have done that." The apology seemed to tangle with regret as it took flight from her throat.

"Why the hell shouldn't you have done that? I intend to take you up on that as soon as I get all of the chores done tomorrow morning. Might even bundle you up, carry you out of bed, put you in my truck, and take you with me to do all the chores." He reveled in her delighted grin. "That's how much I miss you, sugar."

"I miss you all the time, too, but you have to work, and Natalie said …" she trailed off again.

"Natalie said what?" Brock figured Hope and Natalie would eventually come to blows. Nat was as bullheaded as they came. She'd wanted to out-do every one one of her brothers her whole life. It ate at her when she couldn't. Every newcomer to the ranch had to prove their worth in her eyes. She wanted to go up against them to prove her dominance, as stupid as that was. Brock loved his cousin, but he didn't always like her very much. He sure as hell would have words with her the next day over whatever she'd said to Hope. Natalie's stubborn refusal to ever be outdone irked Brock to no end, and her constant need for people to think she was important was ridiculous. If she wanted to tangle with Hope, he'd put a stop to it, quickly.

"Nothing. She was being a bitch, but she was right. I shouldn't ask you to be here more. I have to stop being a big baby."

"Stop it, right now." Brock demanded. "You are my baby, but I've never known you to act like one. Living here is entirely different than living at Gypsy Beach. I don't feel like I prepared you for it before we moved. Feels like we've been living in a whirlwind since we decided to get married before we were ever really engaged." He chuckled at his own impatience to cover the regret that still ate at him. He'd pushed her into this.

"I'm just glad you're here now." Her arms squeezed him tighter. She buried her face against him and mumbled something into his chest.

My God, she was adorable. How the hell had he gotten so lucky? "What was that, sugar? I couldn't quite make it out, but I'm pretty sure you just said, 'Brock, take me to bed and have your way with me.'"

A fit of giggles overtook her. He was quite certain angels couldn't sound any sweeter than her giggling … or her moans of pleasure at his hands. "Well, now, I do wish I'd said that, but I actually said, 'how was the bull sale thing?'"

He brushed a kiss on her beautiful lips. It was so damn easy when they were finally together to pretend that nothing at all was wrong. To leave the endless amounts of snow, cattle, and mutual misery outside their door while they drowned whatever sorrow the day had provided in each other. Having no desire to discuss the sheer number of people he'd encountered that had something to say about his old man, he decided to put his day to rest. His wife was in his arms, on their couch, and staring up at him sweetly. They were going to talk and sort through everything. He'd figure out some way to hear her out, even if he couldn't move them back until spring.

Nothing else mattered at that moment but being together. Giving in, he dipped his tongue into the confection of her mouth, so damn sweet and always hungry for him. His hands made quick work of getting up the sweatshirt she'd pulled on while he nibbled his way to the hollow of her throat. Her body writhed and, "Yes," hissed from her lips.

Why couldn't he read her mind as well as he could read her delectable little body? That would make everything so much easier. His rope-callused hands grazed her slender waist and then he cupped her breasts, fevered and full. To his delight, her back arched in invitation and her nipples immediately pebbled in compliance. "Oh, you are hungry aren't you, sweetie? So hungry for me."

His cock throbbed out its adamant approval against the thin yoga pants she was wearing. Somewhere in the recesses of his mind he tried to remember that letting himself get distracted by their mutual hunger *was* the problem. They started kissing, she started moaning, and all talking was quickly forgotten. The reminder faded when the soft purr of desire sounded in his ear. Damn, but she was beautiful. Finally able to eat real meals instead of existing on Ramen trying to keep her bookstore afloat, she'd developed the sexiest curves he'd ever seen. His mind offered him stunning imagery of her a few pounds thicker, her breasts and hips more full, with a sense of contentment existing deep within her.

"I need you." Her breathy plea shot straight to his groin like a siren's song he had no hope of denying. He groaned in anticipation. Their talk, the movie, their dinner, it could all just wait. They needed this. His body craved hers. He'd had a shit day. This would make everything better. His muscles ached for her touch. His tongue thirsted for her nectar. She satiated him and indulged his every greedy desire. He needed the fulfillment that only came from satisfying her. She needed his temptation, and he could no longer exist without the salvation that only came from his wife. Life itself could just fuck off for a little while. His wife needed something only he could provide. She was so sweet to everyone and yet so damn sexy all for him. Complete perfection wrapped up in the most beautiful package he could ever have imagined with an innocent little sex kitten grin to complete her intoxicating seduction. He was about to show her who she belonged to.

Stripping her of the sweatshirt, he sat up. "Come here to me, darlin'. Let me love you." He straddled her legs over his. Her body rolled and her right nipple brushed over his lips in invitation. He nipped at it, drawing a hungry moan and another decadent roll from her body. Up and down, she ground against the rock hard bulge tenting the fly of his jeans. The lips of her pussy separated around him. Fabric of clothes that were completely unnecessary frustrated him.

Jerking the elastic band of the yoga pants down, he froze when she cringed and gasped. "My God, what happened to you?" Eyes goggling, he studied a large, purple bruise marring her right hip. The skin was raw. He gently ran his fingertips over the swollen knot under the bruise.

Hope stared dejectedly down at her injured hip. It had been throbbing right up until the moment Brock wrapped her up in the substantiality of his arms. His safety and love had eased the pain.

"I slipped in the front yard and landed in ice-covered manure. There was a cow. It was gross!" She buried her face in his neck. She didn't really want to recount the events of her day. He eased her yoga pants back up over her backside. She'd never known Brock to redress her.

When he finished, he cradled the nape of her neck in his hand. "I'm so sorry, sweetheart. We can't seem to win for losing, can we? You sure you're up to this now?"

As there was nothing Hope wanted more than to drown the misery of her day in her husband's gorgeous, overly-muscled body, that question was entirely unnecessary. "Please." She'd beg if she had to.

"Hold on tight." He braced his arm under her backside and stood with her wrapped around his chest.

"Where are we going?"

"Shh, I've got ya."

Hope nuzzled against him and let him carry her down the hall towards their bedroom. The timer on the kitchen oven halted his progress. Sure, *now* it decided to work.

"Let's not burn the pizza." He turned the oven off and then continued their trek to the bedroom.

"Yeah, since I'm incapable of making dinner without burning it." Aware that she was being pouty, she ordered herself to buck up. What was wrong with her lately, anyway?

"Hush. First of all, you need to give yourself a break. Secondly, you need to let me take of you."

"That sounds perfect." A contented sigh slipped from her lips as he laid her in their bed and eased the pants off of her legs completely. That was much better than him redressing her. Heated blood surged through her body from the hungry gaze in his eyes as he dispensed with her panties as well. His gentle love flooded warmth throughout her as he brushed tender kisses over the bruise.

"Poor thing." His hot breath caressed the marking, bringing her relief. "I'm so sorry you fell, but I promise you, darlin', I'm about to make everything feel better." Making quick work of his own clothes, he crawled up over her body keeping his weight on the mattress and off of her.

Groaning in elation, Hope could no longer even feel the ache the bruise left behind. The needy pressure between her legs was far more demanding. When she was in the safety of his arms, in their bed, in the radiating heat that carried the woodsy leather scent of him to her lungs, the consuming loneliness evaded completely. Peace settled her soul. Arching her back in desperate hunger, her body rolled against his. Every spot their skin touched ignited. Electricity amped the need between them.

"Be still for me, sugar. Let me take care of you."

Obeying, she kept her eyes locked on his. Concern and love fought for dominance in their hazel depths. She wished he wouldn't look so worried. Being cared for was all she needed. This would mend every stupid, annoying thing she'd endured that day.

With tender practiced gentleness, he cradled her in his arms and began at her shoulder with open mouth suckled kisses. A breathy gasp escaped her when he indulged her right nipple with the rough caress of his tongue. He sucked away the stiffening hunger that made her ache. Pulling away momentarily, he stared down at her in the glow of the lamp light he'd turned on in their room. Frantic for more, she fought not to whimper.

"You are so damn gorgeous, Hope. I can't stop looking at you. My God, I need you, darlin'. I've needed you all fucking day. This was all I could think about." He lowered his head and drew on her left breast this time. The pressure was exquisite.

"Yes," panted from her lungs as she simply allowed herself to do nothing but feel. Every sucking draw sent lightning bolts of pleasure directly to her pussy. Her mind shut down its incessant psychoanalysis of herself and the fretful worry that appeared at a moment's notice. She succumbed to his reverent care. Liquid heat seeped from her slit. She was so anxious for him to banish her fears completely. "Brock, now, please."

The voracity of his moan said he had no intention of making her wait for his pleasure. His fingers glided down her abdomen, seeking the heat with magnetized force. He circled her navel, making her wriggle. Her body tensed for him.

"You wet for me, baby?"

She felt his finger part her lips as he sought the source of the fevered heat permeating her body.

"Oh, yeah. So wet for me. That's my girl." He pressed deeper. Her body drew him in, and her eyes closed as she allowed herself to do nothing but feel.

Ardent hunger drove Brock. Restoration of their souls was his singular goal. She was his. Every tender tremble of her delectable body made lust surge through his veins and rack rapidly in his groin. Her breasts were swollen larger than he'd ever seen them before. Her sweet little pussy tightened around his fingers. "Feels good doesn't it, sweetie? That's what you needed. I know."

"Brock, please," she begged again.

A thundered groan ripped from his lungs as he fucked her thoroughly with his fingers. His cock longed to trade places with them, but she needed to be set free over and over again. He wasn't leaving that bed until she collapsed under him in completed pleasure. "Want me to let you come, darlin?"

"Please." The throaty plea shivered from her lungs.

His cock throbbed its approval. He knew precisely what she needed. Keeping his fingers deep within her satin channel, he slicked his thumb with the nectar, preparing her for him, and gently caressed the hood of her clitoris. She shook with the need, so hungry for all he could provide. "That's it. Come, sugar. Just let it come for me. I've got you. I'm right here."

Her breath washed from her lungs. She writhed and came on his command. Nothing would ever be as astounding as watching her body tense and pitch in rhythm, shaking as he freed her of every constraint that shackled her soul.

"Turn over on your side for me, sweetheart. I need you." He guided her to her left side to avoid accidentally hurting her bruised right hip. There was no time for patience or finesse. Too much was at stake. Need clawed at his resolve, and her desperation was palpable between them. "So damn beautiful." He slid his right hand down her side then used his fingertips to trace the curves of her luscious ass.

"Now. Please." That begging of hers was always his undoing. How could anything that sweet be so needy for him? He had no idea, but he was certain he'd never deserve the heavenly angel laying beside him anxious for him to stake his claim. God himself had stepped in to bring them together, and Brock would care for her constantly.

Gently, he spread her legs with his right thigh. "I've got you, sugar. I'm gonna make everything better."

When she pressed back against him, a moan rumbled from low in his gut. Gripping himself, he ran the head of his cock between her lips, drenching himself in her juices. Her body gave another needy writhe, and he pierced through her tightened opening, almost losing himself in the ecstasy of it all.

His muscles tensed, and his jaw clenched as he ordered himself not to let go until she did. Making a deep thrust, he concentrated on the rhythm of her need. With satiating pressure, he built her slowly, thoroughly, hungrily. She needed to know who she belonged to, needed to feel his all-consuming love. Purpose and contentment pervaded his soul. He was put on this earth to love her. This was all that mattered. He thrust deeply then pulled away again, and again he took her thoroughly.

"That's it. God, so good, sugar. You feel so fucking good." He rocked her body with his own, taking more, going deeper with each pass until they existed as one.

She trembled against him. Her pussy nursed his cock, so hungry for his cum he was certain he was going to lose his mind. "Not yet, darlin'. Not yet. Be a good girl and let it build for me. You're gonna come with me this time."

"Oh, God! Yes!" She met his every thrust, her body anxious and primed for release. Desperation roiled in his balls. He pumped harder, greedy for her.

When he couldn't deny himself any longer, he brushed his fingertips over her pussy, gathering her dew, then teased her mouth with his fingers. "Suck 'em for me, darlin'." She complied, drawing his fingers in her mouth and sucking ravenously. Primal tension sizzled through his veins as he watched her taste herself from his fingers.

"That's it." He pulled them away when she'd slicked them enough for his purposes and gently stroked over her clit, back and forth, until she tensed against him, and her body bowed taut. "Come," he ordered in a ragged guttural command.

She came with a gasped cry of his name. Hot cum bathed her walls with everything he was. The tedium of their world drown in his potent release. Still trembling against him, Brock eased from the bed and rejoined her on her other side to keep her from laying on her bruised hip. He drew her up on his chest. "That better, sweetie?"

There she was. His sweet giggle spilled from her kiss-swollen lips as she nuzzled against him, sated and happy as if nothing had gotten her down. Bone-deep satisfaction radiated throughout his musculature. The scathing remarks he'd heard about his father, the biting cold, the endless snow, the damn bull that had gotten a piece of him, they could all go to hell. He didn't give a damn. She was in his arms, in their bed, warm, safe, his. Contentment joined the satisfaction in his veins.

"So much better," she sighed.

"Now, how about that pizza and a movie? Not gonna lie. I'm starving."

"Me too."

"Stay put for me." Sliding quickly from the bed, he bundled her up in the covers, threw on a pair of flannel pajama pants, and headed to the kitchen. Damn cold tile floor bit at his feet. He had to do something about the heater. Piling pizza onto paper plates, he grabbed two cans of root beer, retrieved the movie, and returned to bed.

He reveled in her grin, but the gathering storm at the beginning of *Sweet Home Alabama* was all too symbolic. Brock debated pausing the movie and trying to get her to talk, but he didn't want to ruin the moment. She was naked and bundled up in his arms, contentedly eating. His mind was still busy recalling the perfection of satisfying her, the way she trembled and called out his name when she climaxed, the way her body felt in his arms as she gave herself over to the sensations only he could provide, the palpable love they shared. The guilt over not demanding that they talk and figure everything out remained at bay. They could stay up late and talk after the movie was over. Settling on that idea, he dug into the pizza.

Just as Reese Witherspoon was heading to Pigeon Creek to demand that Josh Lucas divorce her, someone pounded on the front door. Bolting upright, Brock pulled on a shirt. His heart thundered in his chest. The knock was urgent. Something was wrong.

"Who is that?" she demanded.

Brock watched the fear returned to Hope's beautiful emerald eyes. She quickly threw on her robe and followed him to the front hall.

"Don't know, sugar, but stay right there for me." According to Austin, Saddlebacks, the only restaurant in town, would be jumping that night. The local pub was the only decent-sized watering hole between the Wyoming line and Lincoln, and there were plenty of cowboys heading home from the bull sale wanting to get in out of the cold and use whiskey and women for warmth. The whole damn state knew where Camden ranch was. It was the largest ranch in five counties. The worry that some idiot might've come to the ranch looking for him because of his father's mistakes made him sick. Keeping Hope safe was all that mattered.

Another knock shook the front door. Debating grabbing his pistol, Brock flung it open. "What the hell?" His tone bled quickly to concern as he took in Uncle Ev, Grady, Austin, Natalie, and Luke's demeanor.

"Gilbert's barn and stables caught fire. They need our help getting the stock moved and the horses out. We need to go now!" Ev urged.

"How the hell did a barn go up in flames in the middle of three feet of snow?" Brock demanded as he quickly located his coat and his boots.

"If I were a betting man, I'd say their idiot kid was smoking out there again near the lighter fluid or the gasoline." Austin rolled his eyes. "Gilbert thinks it was some kids from the high school. That'll be up to the fire department to decide, but they won't be here for an hour so hurry up."

Hope's mouth hung open. Her heart beat rapidly as it slid downward to the vicinity of her feet. Terrorizing fear consumed her with ease. "Brock! I don't understand. Who are the Gilberts, and why do you go when there's a fire? You're a cowboy, not a fire fighter."

"Gilbert's ranch is the next ranch over, sweetheart, and there isn't a fire department in Pleasant Glen. They have to come from the county. It's thirty miles away from here. Takes too long to get here even when there's not snow all over the roads. I'll be fine. Just sit tight. I'll call you when it's over."

With that, Brock sank his left foot in his boot, and headed towards the door.

"Wait! I want to go with you!" Hope knew as soon as she made the demand she would be denied.

"You're staying right here. You're already hurt." He grasped her shoulders. His touch was forceful and laced with urgency. It only served to further terrify her. His kiss matched his tone, gruff and worried. "I love you. It'll be a while before I get home. Go on to sleep."

She watched him go. A riptide of emotion overtook her. What kind of town didn't have a fire department? This place was ridiculous! Did anyone in this town ever think that maybe they should hire firefighters and build a freaking station? What if Brock got hurt? What happened then? She couldn't do it. She couldn't lose anyone else. The abandonment that had presided over her entire life took hold with ease. The chokehold of existing without her parents, without anyone that wanted her, barraged her entire being.

She began to pace. What happened if he wasn't okay? Her entire world hinged on him being all right, and that realization made her even angrier.

Cows, and poodles, moronic mailmen, and bitchy women with their nose in everyone's business, ovens, and cow shit, and coffee makers, and missing lingerie, and no fire department, and never seeing her husband, it all weighted her entire body. Where the hell had they moved, the wild west? This wasn't at all how this night was supposed to go. They were supposed to talk. They were supposed to reconnect. He wasn't supposed to be out fighting fires. The entire earth was covered in snow and yet there was a fire. How did that even happen?

She longed for the beach, her friends, her bookstore, the warm sun on her face, days when Brock showed up at her door with coffee from Mac and Molly's coffee shop. When he could take a day off work and hang out with her. When the weekends were filled with playful banter and teasing laughter, long conversations, and eventually kisses that led to indescribable passion. She even missed her aunt's constant disdain. At least that was familiar. Nothing here made sense to her. And that made her madder than anything else. She'd made it through college with an English Lit degree in three years. How fucking smart did you have to be to figure this ridiculous place out?

She tried to tell herself that she was being selfish. That these people might lose their livelihood, and animals were in danger. The frustration won out with ease. Guilt was no longer a satisfactory bastion against the uprising of resentment. The terror demanded to be felt. Chills quaked from deep within her. Her teeth began chattering. Reaching feebly, she slung the blankets she'd left on the floor over her body. Why was she always so cold? Her chest ached. Her body felt numb except for the cramps settling low in her abdomen and the bruise on her hip that radiated with pain again. The pizza she'd eaten churned in her stomach. Another round of nausea set in. What was wrong with her? Everything. Everything felt wrong, and she wanted to go home.

Chapter Seven

It was nearing three in the morning when Brock eased inside his home. His heart ached as his gaze landed on Hope curled up on the sofa. Her eyes were swollen and red, and it wasn't because she'd been sleeping. She sat up and raced into his arms. Her frantic grasp crushed his soul.

"Are you okay?!"

"I'm fine, sweetie. Let me get a shower. I'm covered in soot and mud. Barn and stables were gone by the time we got there. Melted snow actually helped but it was a fucking mess. We got the fire put out and the cattle loaded up in trucks and moved. Damn near took the house. They lost a horse." Regret weighted the exhaustion already tugging at his eyelids. He tried to remain alert as he slipped his hand to the nape of her neck. She felt warm, but was shivering against him.

"I was scared. I don't understand how there isn't a fire department! That's insane." The fear perforated the frustration in her tone. It was more than he could withstand. Why couldn't he catch a fucking break lately? Moving her up here and taking over his portion of the ranch wasn't supposed to be this hard. He assumed the fear was what had her shaking in his arms.

"I know. I'm sorry, sugar. Let's go to bed, okay? I'm exhausted. Let me hold you and get you to sleep. I have to get up and run the feed trucks in a little while. After that, we can talk."

Hope tried to wait until Brock was out of the shower but she had to use the bathroom ... now! There was only one bathroom in their home. She paced and tugged at her hair, but it was no use. Flinging open the door, she called herself crazy for gazing longingly at a toilet. "Brock, I really have to pee."

Sticking his head out from behind the curtain, he yawned and then stared at her like she was actually insane. "So go, darlin'. I've been aware that you peed for years now. I sure as hell don't give a damn. The little dance you're doing there is cute, but unnecessary."

Trying to convince herself that there was no shame in it, she proceeded. A steady heat had been glowing in her cheeks already. Her blush simply added to it. *He is your husband, after all.* Before that thought could console her, she cringed in pain from the burning sensation. *Oh no. That was definitely not normal.* Too exhausted and emotional to say anything, she finished and crawled into bed, praying that whatever was wrong would just go away on its own.

Her hopes were dashed when she was back in the bathroom 15 minutes later. Completely exhausted, Brock hadn't even stirred when she'd gotten up again.

An hour later, fever shook her body. Downing two Extra-strength Tylenol, she prayed the fever would break. Finally, she broke out in a sweat and managed to sleep for a little while.

When she next awoke, she rushed to the bathroom. Brock was already gone, and she had to go to the doctor, now. She was fairly certain she had a bladder infection, but a host of other issues taunted her attempt at logic. Being good at Biology had provided her too much knowledge on the human body. Bladder infections could spread. They could become septic. Peeing often was a sign of other more horrible things. On the verge of a complete meltdown, she dressed quickly, bundled up in her coat and gloves, and made a large bottle of water. Shaking her head, she poured the water down the sink. She knew she should try to flush the infection out, but she was going to be driving for a long while to get to the doctor. She may have used the bathroom in the vicinity of her husband the night before, but she would not pull off in the snow to relieve herself.

Chapter Eight

Heading out into the freezing cold air, Hope debated. Brock was on Cinder, his beloved horse, working their cattle and the Gilbert's. His truck was parked near the house. She'd never driven a vehicle that large, but she wasn't going to bother Jessie with this, plus she had to learn to drive in snow. Brock would just have to get over it.

Galled by the existence of the entire ranch itself and exhausted from the fever, she climbed up in the truck, thanked the Lord that no more snow had fallen the night before, and slowly drove along the dirt path that led to the gates of Camden Ranch.

Every muscle in her body ached, but she kept them tight, terrified she would hit a patch of ice and careen to her death. Thoughts of the wreck that killed her parents wouldn't leave her be. Fevers always made her anxious. When her thoughts drifted from death by car accident, she longed for her doctor back in Gypsy Beach. The one that always assured her whatever she was experiencing was normal and could be taken care of. The one whose office was only ten minutes from her house and on a pavement road in a complex of other offices. The way things were supposed to be, her mind insisted contentiously.

An hour later, due to her painfully slow speed, she finally reached the main road. "Thank God," she breathed as she turned onto the pavement. She debated stopping and using the library's bathroom, but didn't want to park and have to back out in the truck. The streets had been cleared, but the parking lots were difficult to traverse. The library wouldn't be opened that day, but not because she was spending it with her husband. She tried to care, but couldn't access anything beyond fevered frustration at that moment.

Urgently, she picked up speed and hoped that Natalie wasn't lying to her, and that she wouldn't need to have made an appointment. Now, she just had to find the office.

Another thirty minutes passed, and she hadn't seen any kind of office or any piece of land identified as the McElroy's. Passing yet another rural road marker, she slowed and turned the truck on the desolate road. She had to back up and pull forward three times to execute the turn in Brock's large truck. Attempting to swallow down ardent frustration, she headed back towards town with her eyes trained on the sides of the road in an effort to see the doctor's office. She was going to wet her pants any moment. Wouldn't that be great fodder for gossip all over this stupid town? Brock Camden's wife is incontinent.

Suddenly, she tried to recall when she'd stopped referring to herself as Hope and had started identifying only as Brock's wife. Lost in that despondent thought, her heart leapt into a panicked sprint when she glanced in the rearview mirror and saw the blue lights flashing behind her. *Oh my God! I can't get a ticket. I've never gotten a ticket before.* She'd never even been pulled over before. Terrified to ease the truck off the side of the road lest she slide down an embankment, she simply stopped the car and let the panic consume her. Remembering that Brock and Austin always referred to the Sheriff's Deputy as Barney Fife because they said he was as self-righteous as they came collided with thoughts of what Brock would say when she revealed the ticket she was probably about to receive.

She lowered the driver's side window and shivered from the freezing cold on her fevered face.

"License and registration, ma'am." The deputy demanded.

"Yes, sir." She swallowed harshly and fished her wallet out of her purse. She didn't have a Nebraska license yet. That was another thing Brock kept putting off.

Handing over her North Carolina license, she prayed that the insurance card Brock had on the truck would somehow magically appear in her wallet, but magic didn't seem to be on her side either. Leaning, she popped open the glove box, but there was no registration to be found.

"Um, my husband has the insurance cards, but I swear the truck *is* insured."

"You're Brock Camden's wife aren't you?"

"Yes, sir." She wondered if that was going to be an asset at this point. The Camden cousins used to tease Deputy Fife, or whatever his actual name was, all through school.

"Brock know you're out in his truck?"

Irritation fed the anger radiating in her weary body. "I do not need my husband's permission to drive *our* truck," she spat.

"Maybe not, but to drive in my county, Missy, you do need a legal license and registration."

"My license is legal. It's just not a Nebraskan license."

"You moved to Camden ranch weeks ago, plenty of time to get a new license. I'm calling this in."

Hope shifted uncomfortably and tried to wiggle the snap of her jeans away from her aching bladder. She wished she'd learned some old Gypsy curses from her father. They would come in handy just then. "Look, I'm on my way to the doctor's office. I got lost. Could you just write me a ticket or whatever you're going to do so that I can go? It's urgent."

"Doc Moore's office is three miles that way." He pointed the direction they were currently facing. "If you were coming from the ranch, you drove past it. Then you made an illegal turn in the middle of the road, which is reckless driving, and you were doing 45 in a 30. Seems to me you were trying to go somewhere quick. Does Brock know where you are, or maybe you weren't coming from Camden Ranch? Maybe you're somewhere you had no business being and were trying to escape before he figures out what kind of woman you are."

Hope gasped in shock and then ground her teeth to keep from assaulting a police officer. "Look, Deputy Fife," she sneered. "I told you I got lost. I don't know how to get to the doctor's office. I *am* the kind of woman that is sick and needs a doctor! What does any of that have to do with Brock?"

The Deputy narrowed his eyes. "If I were you, *Ms.* Camden, I'd hold my tongue before I impound this truck and take you in. Then we'll see just what Brock thinks of that. Serves him right, marrying a girl that's just as pompous and loud-mouthed as he is."

Her good sense returned to her, and Hope bit her tongue to keep from arguing. She might have been irked with their blessed ranch, but Brock was humble and kind to most everyone. She recalled the stories that the would-be deputy wanted to play football in Middle School with Brock, Grant, and Luke. He didn't make the team and was relegated to water boy. Then Brock and his horse Lucky had beaten him numerous times in young rodeo competitions. The grudge was clearly still being held.

By the time the deputy ran her license and plates and phoned Sheriff Wilheim for good measure, Hope had broken out in a cold sweat. She swayed in her seat from the fever and desperation to get to a bathroom. The Deputy tore three tickets from his pad. "One for reckless driving and speeding, another for driving without insurance, and one for driving with an out of state license. Sheriff says if Brock'll come by the office with proof of insurance he'll waive the insurance one. When you get your license renewed, we'll drop that one as well. After that little fit you pitched, I told the Sheriff not to be so light on you, but he's been friends with the Camdens for years. He's thrilled Brock's back in town. Don't expect to be treated so nicely when I become sheriff," he smarted.

Unable to believe her current life, Hope stared in shock at not one, not two, but three tickets. How did a person go from having a perfect driving record to being the recipient of three traffic tickets? Certain that she was going to wet her pants if she didn't get to restroom soon had her nodding her understanding. "Okay. Thanks." She shifted the truck into drive.

"I shouldn't let you drive without insurance, ya know?"

Closing her eyes and drawing a deep breath that made her wince, Hope attempted to summon calm. "I really appreciate you letting me go. I promise I'll bring the insurance card to the sheriff's office, and I will get my license renewed. I'm really feeling very sick. Could I please go … sir?" She opened her eyes and attempted a pleading look.

"Fine, but mind your speed."

"I will. I promise."

Hope checked the mile gauge. Anger gave way quickly to embarrassment over the incident. Brock would never want to teach her to drive in the snow when the first time she'd attempted it she'd ended up with three traffic tickets.

Her bladder gave another urgent cramp and another round of nausea built in her stomach. She longed to double over in the seat. She'd have to worry about the tickets later. There were far more pressing matters at hand. Three miles. That was actually helpful information. As she neared the three mile mark she noted an old brown one story building that had three garage bay doors on the side. Surely, this wasn't the doctor's office. It appeared to have been some kind of mechanic shop at one time.

Whatever it was, there were cars parked outside, meaning if she was lucky, there might be a bathroom inside. Deciding she wasn't above begging to use the restroom, she threw the truck into park. When her feet hit the ground several feet below her, she winced as her hip reacted to the jolt. This was not her day, or her week, or her month it seemed.

Ignoring the protest of her hip, she raced through the front doors and halted abruptly. It was indeed a waiting room full of people. The front desk had been constructed out what must've been an old kitchenette. Glancing around frantically, Hope didn't see a restroom anywhere.

Heading towards the woman seated at the counter, she fought not to cross her legs once she'd arrived. "Um, is this Dr. Moore's office?"

The woman, whom Hope assumed was Mindy, the receptionist, studied Hope like she was concerned she'd had suffered a blow to the head. "That's what it says right there." She pointed to an out of the way door near the back, what would have at one time led to the garage bays.

"Sorry, didn't see that. Um, I need to see the doctor but … uh …" she leaned closer, "I'm pretty sure I have a bladder infection. I really need to use the restroom before I sign in."

"Aren't you Brock Camden's wife or something?"

Weary of being asked that question, Hope sighed. "Yes, I'm Brock's wife. Could you please tell me where the restroom is?"

"Sure, but you're gonna have to fill out a bunch of paperwork."

"Okay, but I have to go to the bathroom, now!"

"Through that door, turn right, walk down the hallway. Doc's hound dogs are back there so try not to wake 'um. You'll see it on your left. I put some apple potpourri back there."

"Thanks." Hope raced through the door and almost ran head long into a man in a white coat with a name tag identifying him as Dr. Moore. "Sorry, sir." Hope whimpered. "Bathroom?" She pointed to her right as Mindy had directed.

"Yes ma'am. It's that way. I'm sorry I wasn't expecting someone to be coming through the door so exuberantly. I didn't bump into you, did I? You're not hurt?" Dr. Moore was a kind old man with a pot belly, white-grey hair, and deep blue eyes that reminded Hope of Santa Claus.

She half-grinned and half-grimaced. "I'm fine. Sorry, I was the one that rushed through. It's my fault." She was out of time. She had to go now. Backing away from the doctor she turned and sprinted past two sleeping hound dogs as she barreled into the restroom.

Brock fished his buzzing cell phone out from under the full chaps he'd put on to ward off the cold. Smiling, he was certain Hope was calling to see when he'd be back home. His brow furrowed. It wasn't Hope. He didn't recognize the number. "Hello?"

"Mr. Camden, this is Deputy Sheriff Clarke Newsome."

Brock rolled his eyes and slowed Cinder to a trot. "Clarke, I've known you since you were five. Can all of the Deputy Sheriff shit. What do you want?"

Huffing and puffing as only he could, Clarke bellowed, "I'll have you know, Brock, that I just pulled your wife over for reckless driving, driving with an out-of-state license, and operating an uninsured vehicle on a state road."

"You're so full of it. My wife is in our bed, beautiful, and perfect — and waiting on me." He threw in just to make Newsome jealous.

Clarke laughed haughtily. "I figured as much. You can't even keep up with your own wife. I warned Sheriff Wilheim about you moving back here. You're no better than your father. After she performed a three-point turn in the middle of the highway and got caught traveling 15 miles over the speed limit, your wife told me she was trying to find Doc Moore's office. I wrote her three tickets myself."

"You did what?" Fury scalded Brock's resolve. *How had Hope gotten to town on her own, and why the hell hadn't she called to tell him she was going somewhere?*

"I wrote her three tickets. You'll need to come by the sheriff's office and bring your proof of insurance on your 2013 Ford F-350 dually pick-up, black, license plate number 479KH."

"Yeah, yeah, that's my truck. I get it. I'll be there later. You said Hope was going to the doctor's office?"

"That's what she told me. Probably a lie. Who doesn't know where Doc Moore's office is? You ought to keep an eye on her. She's trouble. I always know."

With a grunt of annoyance, Brock muttered, "Sure, whatever, Clarke. I'll see you in a little while." Kicking Cinder back to life, he galloped towards Ev, Luke, and Austin on the other end of the back fields trying to round up the Gilbert's cattle. *What the hell was wrong with Hope? Why did she need the doctor, and why hadn't she told him she was leaving?* Frantic with worry, he shouted that he had to go back home as he neared Austin. They nodded, and he was off.

After borrowing Grant's truck, he made it to the highway in under twenty minutes. He'd grown up driving trucks all over the ranch. Hell, he was driving the massive feed trucks pulling hay trailers when he was ten. Driving in snow didn't concern him. Whatever was wrong with his wife did. If Clarke had said anything that upset her or had made her sicker because he was being a douchebag, Brock would string him up by his vocal chords and whip his ass so hard the annoying little pipsqueak's tenor voice would be soprano for the rest of his life.

Chapter Nine

Complete mortified and still unable to believe this was how it worked in this doctor's office, Hope carefully carried the cup full of her own urine through the waiting room to Mindy at the front desk as the nurse had instructed her. Without meeting any of the eyes peering at her with a mix of curiosity and disgust, she set the cup on the desk and raced back to the room she'd been assigned. Climbing dejectedly up onto the paper lined exam table, Hope studied the brown paneled walls of the room. It seemed when Dr. Moore set up office in the old fix-it shop they'd used paneling to divide out hallways and rooms. It felt a bit like sitting inside her own house of cards.

"Ms. Camden, we meet again." Dr. Moore bustled in the room chuckling at his own joke.

Hope was far too humiliated over her morning to join in his laughter.

Concern wiped the grin from his face. "Nurse Carmichael tells me you're showing symptoms of a urinary tract infection. Have you been running a fever, dear?"

"Yes, sir. I think that's why I was so cold yesterday, and why I fell asleep and let our dinner burn." *Oh my God, Hope, shut up. That was entirely more information than he needed.*

Dr. Moore nodded. "Well, the wind and weather can be a little rough on a newcomer until they've gotten used to it. It's normal to feel tired while your body is adjusting to winters here." Before she could respond, he shook his head. "Forgive me, that was presumptuous of me. I'm certain you've figured out that everyone knows everything about everyone else in this town. I already know you married Brock Camden and that you'd moved to the ranch. Perhaps, I should have started with welcoming you to Pleasant Glen." He offered Hope a very kind smile, and a sense of calm managed to work through her anxiety-ridden body.

"Oh, it's all right. I know everyone knows I'm married to Brock and living on the ranch. Um, while I'm here, could I go ahead and get a renewal on my Ortho-novum prescription?" For some unfathomable reason, she just kept blurting things out. Sinking her teeth into her tongue she ordered herself to calm.

"I don't see why not. I'll need to do a quick pelvic examination first."

Hope fought not to whimper. She didn't want this strange man with hound dogs in his office performing any kind of exam on her, even if he did seem very kind. Swallowing down the tension that settled in her throat, she called herself a baby for the tenth time since setting foot in the office. She wanted Brock.

"How long have you been taking Ortho-novum?"

"Since I was 18." She tried not to blush, but felt her cheeks flood with another round of heat. "I was put on it for irregular periods." *Shut up, Hope! No one cares about that.*

"I understand. No need to be embarrassed, dear. I try not to believe anything I hear and only half of what I see." Dr. Moore stood and placed his stethoscope on her chest. "Deep breath." He listened for a moment and then gave her another smile. "And you're happy with Ortho-Novum for birth control as well as treating your irregular periods?"

"Yes, sir." *There. That's good. Just answer the questions like a normal human being.*

"Any other concerns other than the frequent urination and fever?"

"Um, no, everything is fine other than that. Well, my stomach hurt all afternoon and evening, but I'd had a horrible day. I fell in a manure pile." She cringed. Clearly, she would never be capable of keeping her mouth shut.

When he finished listening to her heart, he went back to the chart the nurse had started for her and nodded. Moving back to her, he reclined her on the table and pressed around her abdomen. "Would you mind unsnapping your jeans for me just a little?"

"Oh, sure." She wondered if she should ask for a nurse to be present. Somehow, in this tiny town, in this tiny doctor's office that used to be a mechanic shop, things like that seemed unnecessary. She eased her pants down just a little so he could press around her bladder.

"Hmm, interesting. You said you fell asleep yesterday afternoon?"

Hope nodded.

"When you say you were sick to your stomach, did you vomit?"

"No, sir. I don't think I have a stomach virus or anything."

"And when was your last menstrual cycle, Hope?"

"Oh," she thought back, "I guess about a month ago. I'm down to my last few placebo pills, so I should be starting any time now."

"How did you get that?" Breaking from his current line of questioning, Dr. Moore gestured to the bruise evident on her right hip.

"I fell yesterday. I slid on a patch of ice and landed right there. That's how I ended up in a manure pile."

"You're certain you fell? If there's anything you need to tell me Hope, whatever you say in here won't leave these walls."

Sitting up, Hope tried to fathom what on earth he was asking her. "I swear. I fell yesterday on a patch of ice in our front yard. What on earth are you talking about?"

His interrogating eyes studied her closely. She crossed her arms over her chest.

"I'm not lying to you!" Her vehemence seemed to convince him.

"You certainly don't seem to be. Bad memories I suppose."

"Bad memories?" Hope mind spun rapidly. "Wait. You mean. You think Brock's like his father?"

"I never said that."

"But that is what you were asking me. Dr. Moore, my husband is kind, and sweet, and good, and wonderful to me and to everyone else." Brock was all of those things, so why was she so frustrated with him lately? It wasn't really his fault this town was insane.

"I am sorry if I implied that. It's my job to care for this community. I try not to make assumptions, but I saw Brock and his mother in here numerous times for bumps and bruises that they didn't get from falling, even though that's what his mother always told me."

"Brock would never hurt me."

"Understood. Please accept my apologies."

Hope nodded, but wasn't certain she did forgive the accusations towards her husband.

"All right, dear, I'm not going to put you through a vaginal exam today. I'm going to get you a sample of something that will ease the pain and urgency to urinate frequently. I'll write you a prescription for that as well as soon as we have the results from your urine sample. Let me go see what's keeping the nurse with those, and I'll get you the pills that will ease the pain."

"Thank you." Hope sat up and tried to button her jeans without pressing on her bladder.

She sat there staring at the brown walls, wondering how to regain her equilibrium. She was still frustrated with Brock about not letting her drive and never being home, but knew she shouldn't be. She may hate this town, but to him it would always be home. Gypsy Beach probably seemed odd to him when he'd moved there in high school. The image of the poodles sitting in the beauty shop chairs formed in her mind. Okay, Pleasant Glen was a special kind of crazy, but she tried to see things from his perspective. He'd always been protective of her, even before they were dating. Why couldn't she just be happy again? Guilt, confusion, frustration, and pain swirled in a volatile mass in her stomach. She felt heavy with the weight of it all.

"Hope, baby, are you all right?" Suddenly, he was there. Dr. Moore followed Brock in the room, smiling.

"What are you doing here?" She reached for him. That was all she'd wanted since the night before when her world had come apart when he'd walked out the front door to fight a fire.

His hazel eyes reflected his deep concern as he cradled her in his arms. "I would have been in here sooner. Had to tell Mindy to sit down and shut it because I was coming back here no matter what she thought." He turned to Dr. Moore. "Is she okay? I can take her to St. Elizabeth's."

Hope knew St. Elizabeth's was the hospital in Lincoln. Surely this wasn't that serious.

"I don't think that will be necessary, Brock. By the way, it's good to see you again." He offered Brock his hand. "Um, Hope, dear we're having a hard time locating the specimen you left us. Where did you put it?"

Lifting her head from her husband's chest, she furrowed her brow. "I took it to the front desk like the nurse said to."

Dr. Moore tried to cover his chuckle. "Uh, I believe she meant the nurse's desk, not the front desk. The nurse's desk is at the other end of this hallway. I'll go see if I can find that."

So, she'd carried her own pee through the waiting room for no good reason. Hope fell back against Brock's chest. "How did you know I was here?"

"Clarke called me."

"Who's Clarke?"

"The Sheriff's Deputy. He said he pulled you over for some illegal turn or something. I'm going from here to see

Sheriff Wilheim. I'll get it taken care of. Clarke's an asshat. Don't worry about anything, but what specimen? What's Doc Moore talking about?"

"A urine sample. I think I have a bladder infection." She sighed. "And apparently, I actually carried a cup of my own pee into the waiting room in front of all of those people, and I wasn't supposed to."

Brock gently rubbed her back and planted a kiss on top of her head. "No one cares about that, darlin'. Is this serious? What do we need to do?"

Willing patience from the stale air surrounding her, she wondered how he seemed so capable of not caring what other people thought. She sat back up and shook her head. "I don't think it's too serious. I've had one before."

Dr. Moore returned just then. "The nurse had already located it. Your urine sample doesn't show an infection, but I suspect you do have a very slight one, Hope. We'll send your sample to the lab to be sure, but I'm going to go ahead and treat you. I did test your urine for something else that showed up readily. I don't really think the refill on birth control pills will be necessary. Take these, and I'll get the prescriptions written." He handed Hope a tiny brownish-red pill and a bottle of water.

She downed the pill quickly, anxious for relief. "What do you mean the birth control pills aren't necessary? What showed up readily?"

"Urinary tract infections are quite common in women, especially when they're pregnant. I had a sneaking suspicion that was it. If you haven't yet missed a period yet, you're very early on in the pregnancy. The antibiotic will take care of the infection, so no need to worry. Limit your caffeine. Get lots of rest, and drink lots and lots of water. Tylenol is fine for the fever, and the medication you just took should ease the bladder infection symptoms readily. You caught it early. You should be feeling better by this evening. Take one of those pills every few hours as often as you need them. Instead of the prescription for

Ortho-Novum, I'm going to write you one for prenatal vitamins. If the nausea gets to be too much, I can give you something for that as well."

"Wait! I can't be pregnant. I'm on the pill." Hope's entire world spun off its axis. Brock reached and wrapped his arm around her. Was he actually smiling? Something told her she should be happy. He appeared to be, but the only emotion she could locate was confusion. Everything that had happened the day before, everything she didn't understand about living in Nebraska, everything she didn't know about having a baby overwhelmed her. She gasped for breath. Nothing made sense.

"The pill is only 99% effective, and the fact that you've been on the same one for years might've lessened its effectiveness. Whenever this happens, I generally tell people that the Big Man upstairs must've had other plans."

"Well, it would have been nice if the Big Man upstairs had checked with me first!" Hope couldn't believe what she was being told.

Brock stared at her like she'd just sprouted another head. "Hope," he huffed under his breath. He appeared somewhat shell shocked as well, but she didn't know if it was due to being told that they were very unexpectedly going to have a baby or her reaction to the news.

She eased off the table, anxious to get out of there. She felt suffocated by her own existence. She couldn't breathe.

"Being shocked is completely normal. Take a few days and let it settle in. Remember, no alcohol, lots of rest, good healthy foods, but try not to let this change your marriage. Sex is fine. It's healthy for the two of you, and having a healthy marriage is good for the baby. You're only a few weeks along. There is a reason you get nine months to prepare. I don't do many deliveries anymore. Most women prefer to see an obstetrician in Lincoln. I can recommend one if you'd like." Dr. Moore's grin continued to expand. "Like I said, take some time to let this sink in.

Unless something out of the ordinary happens, you won't need to see another doctor until you've passed the twelve-week mark."

"Could we just have second, Doc?" Brock's plea made Hope feel more ashamed. She focused only on breathing. Everything else was too much just then.

"Of course. I'm going to go get her prescriptions written. They'll be at the front desk whenever you're ready to leave. She needs to start taking that immediately. Take good care of her, and congratulations, you two." With that Dr. Moore left the room.

Tears tracked down her face. She couldn't halt them. She just didn't have the strength.

"Why are you crying, darlin'? I know it's a little earlier than we'd planned, but ..." Panic and elation fought for dominance in Brock's mind. He didn't know what to say. He assumed tears were probably normal, but that didn't make his heart ache less.

"Because, this wasn't supposed to happen yet, and our house is always freezing cold, and the oven doesn't like me, and yesterday, I wanted to shoot the coffe maker, and I fell in cow poop! And people in this town are completely insane, Brock! Completely! And censorship, and I never see you, and now you're going to think that I hate it here just because I'm pregnant. I don't know how to be a mom, but I want to be a good one." Brock watched his wife cradle her own stomach. "I don't know how to do anything, and it's going to need me to know how to do everything. And you won't teach me anything. I don't know how the ranch works, or how to drive in the snow, or what to do with a baby, or why I hate this town, but I know that I do!" Her volume increased with each word until a racked sob consumed her explanation.

Absolutely dumbfounded, Brock held her tighter. He made an attempt at navigating everything she'd just declared. They definitely needed to talk, but not there in the doctor's office. How had he let her be so miserable for so long?

"I don't know what to do," she managed to continue with another haggard draw of breath. "I have to take care of it. I love it."

"*We* will take care of our baby, sweetheart. I'm so sorry. I had no idea you were so miserable. Let's go get the medicine, and go home and talk, okay?"

"I'm scared, and tired, and there are poodles at the beauty shop." She convulsed against him.

Furrowing his brow in complete confusion, he nodded.

"Okay, I know, sugar, but I swear to you I will take care of you and the baby. I'll do whatever you want. If you really hate it here, I'll move you back to North Carolina, okay?" He tried to keep the defeat from his tone.

"I have to go to the bathroom again."

Brock helped her off the table and guided her towards the restrooms. Fantasies of her swollen full of their baby mixed in with the all too real images of her declarations that she hated life on the ranch. If sympathy nausea was a thing, he suddenly had it. "I'll wait right here, darlin'. Go ahead." Worry weighted every chiseled plane of his body.

Still unable to dry her tears of frustrated confusion, Hope whisked down the hallway. She halted suddenly when a dog bound out of the room to her right, barking and growling at her. Her heart flew, and she instinctively wrapped her arms over her abdomen again. Brock was there instantly. He had the dog by the collar.

"Go on, I've got him. He's being obstinate. Doesn't recognize you. I'd never let anything hurt you, sugar. You know that, don't you?" The pain and concern in Brock's tone couldn't quite sooth her shock over being pregnant.

Managing a nod, Hope spun into the women's room. She could still hear Brock and the dog through the thin walls. "Hush," Brock commanded, turning the dogs growls readily to whimpered whines. "That's it." He coaxed. Hope could hear the slight jangle of the dog's collar. Brock must've been petting her. He was so good at everything there. She finally admitted that she was a little jealous. Taking things moment by moment as that was the only real way she could manage currently, she was pleased to discover that the medication Dr. Moore had given her had already eased the pain somewhat.

By the time she returned to the hallway, Brock and the dog were playing tug-a-war with a toy the dog must've supplied. Giving the dog one more pat, Brock stood and brushed a kiss on Hope's cheek. "We'll get everything figured out. I swear to you. Let's get you feeling better first."

"The sheriff's deputy guy wrote me several tickets." Her head fell. Life itself felt too heavy at the moment.

"Yeah, he told me." Brock drew her gently into his protective embrace. "Don't worry about it. I'll go talk to Max. Clarke has two corncobs permanently shoved up his ass sideways. I'll always take care of you, sweetie."

His tender embrace, coupled with the soothing sound of his low, rumbling voice, had her melting against him. Another round of confusion welled inside of her. Everything worried her. Having a fever couldn't be good for the baby. Her fall the day before might've hurt it as well. She drank a lot of coffee. Was that okay? Her job. Brock. The ranch. Her mind spun in too many directions. She couldn't decide what to do first. She was completely overwhelmed with it all. She didn't know how to have a baby or be a good mother. She didn't know how to do anything.

"Let's get you home and into bed. We'll talk, and I'll get Aunt Jessie to make you some of her cure-all soup. Not sure how it works so well, but she made it for all us kids growing up. It always made me feel better." He tightened her in his embrace for a moment, patted her backside, and then released her.

Truthfully, the idea of laying around in bed eating soup and letting her husband tend to her was extremely appealing, but she didn't want Jessie going to any trouble on her behalf.

"I'll be okay. That medicine is already helping. I'm sorry I freaked out."

Brock took her hand. "It's been a rough few weeks, sugar. I should have done a thousand things I didn't do. Let's go home and talk." He guided her back into the waiting room and nodded to a few people he obviously knew. Consumed with her own frustrations and confusion, Hope distractedly wondered what had brought so many people in to the doctor's office that day. It appeared some kind of cold was going around.

She watched Brock pay Mindy for her visit before he guided her out to the parking lot.

"I know it's a little earlier than we thought it would be, sweetie, but I'm excited." Desperation laced his voice, and deep concern darkened his eyes as he halted in the parking lot to study her.

"I'm excited, too ... I think. I'm just really, really scared. I need some things to change, Brock. A lot of things."

"I know. I swear I heard everything you said in there. I think I understand where all of that came from, except maybe the parts about censorship and the poodles. You can explain that later. Just please, let me help you figure out what we want to do. I'll do anything you want. You're all that matters to me. We'll talk all afternoon. I promise."

"Okay." Hope tried to draw in several deep breaths, but the icy air stung her lungs and made her cringe. Without much thought, she pulled the keys out of her purse and headed towards the truck, anxious to get out of the wind.

"Hope, baby, I'm not supposed to let you drive until I go show our insurance cards to Clarke. Come on, let me take care of you. Let me drive you home. I'll get Grant and Austin to come back and get his truck later."

"Brock, that's ridiculous. I keep telling you I am perfectly capable of driving myself places."

"You are perfectly capable, Hope. I'm sorry. I should have taught you to drive in this when I got you up here. Add that to the list of things I screwed up, but I can't let you drive or they'll impound my truck and you could get arrested. I wouldn't put it past Clarke. He gets giddy when he gets to cuff someone. It's kind of sick."

Brock lifted his truck keys from her right hand. She didn't have any fight left in her. She was pregnant, but not allowed to drive. How had something like that happened?

She remained unable to locate her voice as he drove them slowly back to the CVS that for some unfathomable reason everyone still called Wilton's drugs. The Wilton family had sold to CVS years before, according to Jessie. Hope's mind spun again full of the oddities of the tiny town.

"I love you, sugar. Please talk to me."

"I love you, too. I just need to think for a little while." She didn't really know what to say. He loved the ranch. He was born to be a cowboy. The way he handled the animals and the endless work spoke volumes. He never got rattled by it all. He genuinely loved it every part of it.

"Okay, just tell me when you're ready to talk. I'm right here."

Putting the truck into park in the CVS parking lot, Brock was out and standing at her door the next second. He offered her his hand.

"Do you promise to teach me to drive here?"

"That's not going to be necessary if we move back, is it?"

The utter defeat in his tone ate at her. He'd given up everything when he was a kid because his father had lost part of the ranch. Now, because she was giving up, she was going to take it all away again. No. She wouldn't.

Somewhere from deep within her soul her determination made a reappearance. "We're not moving. I need you to help me learn how to live here, but we're not moving."

Shock replaced the dejection that had previously darkened his eyes. "I'll do anything you want, Hope, but know that I really do love driving you to work and taking you places. I love being with you. Sometimes I feel like while we're in the car is the only time we really talk anymore. Not to be a complete pussy, but it's the only time I get to see you smile lately."

She knew that was true. She hadn't even been making an attempt at being happy, not really. She'd just compared their life before to the one they were currently living. When it came up short in her mind, she blamed the town or Brock. They both had some things that had to change. "Well, I still have to know how to get around here."

Her pride was bruised over the tickets, everything that had happened the day before, and she was still in complete shock after finding out she was pregnant just four months after getting married. She did love being in the truck with Brock with no one else hanging around, but she had to try harder to make Pleasant Glen their home.

Chapter Ten

Before they could make their way to the back counter to have the prescriptions filled, an elderly woman halted Brock in the liniment and muscle pain reliever aisle. It was no surprise that the Pleasant Glen CVS had trouble keeping that in stock. Cowboys and cowgirls worked hard, and their muscles were often sore.

"Well, Brock Camden, as I live and breathe, how are you sweetheart?" She reached up and caressed Brock's face. Hope's brow furrowed, but Brock allowed the gesture.

"Mrs. Huffton, how are you, ma'am? This is my wife, Hope. Hope, this is Mrs. Huffton, she was my Sunday School teacher all through elementary school. Uncle Ev told me you'd moved away. I was sorry to hear about Mr. Huffton's passing."

Hope grinned at the woman. The kind twinkle in her eye gave Hope peace.

"Well, thank you for saying so. All part of life, I suppose. It is so lovely to meet you, Hope. I'd heard you'd married, Brock, but I had no idea you'd found such a kind, loving wife. I'm so proud for you."

Hope wondered how Mrs. Huffton knew she was kind and loving.

"I can always tell, dear." Mrs. Huffton answered, as if she could read Hope's thoughts.

"She's perfect. I'm a lucky guy." Brock wrapped his arm around Hope's shoulders.

"I think you're a *blessed* guy, young man. I'm just in town visiting my grandbabies. When this town eventually gets to you and you need a little break, head out to Lincoln and I'll make you both supper. Everyone needs a break every now and then." She winked at Hope, strengthening Hope's suspicion that this woman was actually a mind reader. She reminded her of Molly from Gypsy Beach. Molly was legendary in North Carolina for her soothsaying abilities. Either this woman had Gypsy blood, or Hope's weary anxiety was clearly written on her features. She wondered if Mrs. Huffton somehow knew she was pregnant, too.

"We might take you up on that, Mrs. Huffton. Thanks." Brock smiled. "It was good to see you." He offered her a wave and proceeded back towards the pharmacy area. "It's creepy how she does that mind reading thing, isn't it? We couldn't ever get away with anything in her class," Brock recalled as he handed over the prescriptions to the pharmacist and guided Hope to a chair in the waiting area. "Need anything while we're in town? Looks like they're stocking new romance novels over there." He gestured to the decent sized book section of the CVS. "I haven't seen you read in ages. You used to always have a book with you."

Considering that, Hope was mildly interested in a new book, but she couldn't process anything beyond the fact that she was pregnant. Books had always been her escape. She couldn't figure out why she'd stopped reading after they'd moved. It added to her constantly confused state of being. "I can just get something from the library." She offered up the standard excuse that she repeated to herself often.

Brock racked his brain. The events of the morning tossed tumultuously in his gut. He rather preferred the idea that Hope had been so out of sorts lately because she was pregnant. She *was* shocked. Hell, they were both shocked, but that wasn't the source of her frustration and misery.

If Hope didn't jump at the chance to get a new book, something was definitely wrong, baby or not. He tried to recall the last time he'd seen her curled up on the sofa with one of her books. As he thought back, he couldn't locate any memories of her reading at all in their new home. The endless boxes of books he'd loaded onto their moving van were still sitting unpacked up in the loft. She'd been so thrilled with the upstairs nook and all of the built-in bookshelves when they'd visited the ranch back in September. To his knowledge, she hadn't even been up there since they'd officially moved in.

He missed watching her escape into other worlds via her books. He loved the way she used to bite her bottom lip and how her cheeks glowed pink when she read a steamy love scene from one of her romance novels. He missed the way her eyes danced when she read something that intrigued her. It wasn't something he felt he could ever really have, but he wanted her to have every story she wanted. How did he make her realize that?

He helped Hope stand and watched her disappear to the restroom again. Poor baby. He sure as hell hoped Doc was right and that she was feeling much better soon. Checking his watch, he wondered if it would be shitty of him to take her by the Sheriff's office to give Clarke a piece of his mind, or if he should take her on home and come back to town later. Was delaying their trip home better than having to leave her alone at home again? *Marriage should come with instructions, not that I'd be able to read them,* he thought dejectedly.

Before he could contemplate further, his name bellowed from nearby. He lifted his head and forced a grin. Standing, he offered Sal Cartwright his hand before he shook both of Sal's sons' hands. They'd been toddlers when he'd moved away, but were now both taller than their old man.

"How the hell are ya, son? Ev kept swearing you'd moved back, but I told everybody I wouldn't believe it 'til I saw it myself," Sal laughed.

Brock nodded. "We're back. I can't seem to get off the ranch long enough to see everyone. How's your family?"

"We're good. Matt's heading to Nebraska-Lincoln in the fall, and Taylor here's starting quarterback at Glen High this year." Sal slapped one of his sons on the shoulder.

"Congrats." Brock tried not to think of his own high school football heroics. They'd almost cost him his wife, so his memories were all cast in the shadows of the lies he'd lived his whole life.

"Hey, Holly's at Nebraska-Lincoln, isn't she?" Matt inquired.

This brought a genuine chuckle to Brock's lips. Clearly, Matt had a crush on Brock's youngest cousin, though he doubted Holly would give him the time of day. She was well known for her opinion that cowboys from the Glen weren't what she was looking for. "Yeah, Hol's at Lincoln. She's finishing up her masters, though."

"Maybe I'll give her a call next time's she's home."

It seemed Matt didn't see the age difference as a problem.

Sal rolled his eyes and shook his head. "Worse than a penned bull in the middle of a pack of heifers."

Matt glared at his father as his face reddened dramatically.

Trying not to laugh outright, Brock reached his hand towards Hope when she exited the restroom. "Mr. Cartwright, this is my wife, Hope. Hope, this is one of Uncle Ev's best friends, Sal Cartwright. They've known each other since birth."

"It's nice to meet you, sir," Hope replied automatically.

"You too, darlin', and if this boy gives you any trouble, you let me know." Sal gave her a mischievous wink, but Hope only offered a weary smile as she stole a quick glance at the pharmacist.

"I'm sure they'll be ready soon, sugar." Brock wrapped his arm around her and brushed a kiss on the side of her head. It killed him that she was hurting and there was nothing he could do. She'd announced that she hated it there, but then said they weren't moving back to the beach. If she'd give him half a chance, he'd do better by her, somehow, no matter where she wanted them to live. They were having a baby. He had to make money come spring, but he was determined to hear her out about whatever she needed him to change. He'd figure it all out … somehow.

"Well, we're in to get some udder wash. They're out at Merle's. Now I'll have to pay twice as much. It's nice to meet you, Hope." Sal tipped his hat, but before they could head towards the farming supply aisle, Miles Baxter from the post office barreled through their gathering.

"Mrs. Camden, I've been looking all over town for you. I went to the library, but you're not there. After I went there, I went out to Camden Ranch. Austin and Grant said you were in town. I'm so sorry ma'am. The package was all busted up when I got it. Must'a fallen off the truck and landed in the snow. I tried to dry out them fancy underthings you ordered, but I think you'll have to see if the company will give you a refund. They're torn."

Brock watched his wife turn the approximate shade of the purple lace panty-and-bra ensemble that Miles Baxter held up to reveal what he thought were tears in the fabric. When he pulled apart the crotch of the intentionally open-crotch panties, Brock jerked them out of his hand. Unfortunately, in doing so, he revealed the open slits in the bra meant to showcase her nipples.

Sal ran his hand over his face to keep from laughing outright. His boys cracked up as did half of the drugstore.

Tears welled in Hope's emerald eyes. Time seemed to stand still. Brock didn't know what to say, and suddenly she bolted. Before he could race after her, the pharmacist called, "Hope Camden." He stared down at the lingerie in his hands and attempted to wad it up into a ball before retrieving her medicine. "She needs to take the prenatal vitamins every single day for the duration of the pregnancy. Folic acid is important for a healthy baby," the pharmacy tech offered with entirely too much volume. Brock's head fell in defeat as he managed a slight nod. He turned and stared out into the sea of chuckling cowboys. The fact that his wife had ordered lingerie like that shocked him almost as much as Doc Moore's announcement that she was pregnant. She'd been so out of sorts lately. She wasn't able to handle the insanity of this small town. Besides, he doubted a woman with far more experience than she had would have responded any differently to their lingerie being revealed in the middle of a drug store. He had no idea how to fix this, but she needed him, and he'd be there.

She refused to look at him all the way back to the ranch. He tried feebly to come up with some way to make this better. He was still dumbfounded that she'd ordered lingerie in the first place, and dammit if he wasn't freaking turned on every time he thought about her in the open-crotch panties he'd tried to discreetly drop behind her seat in the truck. His libido wasn't helping him in this case. His mind offered him stunning imagery of her parading around him dressed in the lingerie, of him tonguing her nipples through the cloth, and then pounding into her while she kept those sexy-as-hell panties on, since that's what they were created for. He had no idea what to do *now*, however. Telling her he thought the lingerie was the sexiest thing he could ever have imagined was definitely not the route to take at the moment.

"Hope, sugar, please talk to me," he tried again.

Another round of tears cascaded down her cheeks as she shook her head vehemently. Before he could even put the truck in park when he pulled into their driveway, she flew into the house.

He fought not to bang his head against the steering wheel. Mindy had given them the prescription for prenatal vitamins. The entire town now certainly knew she was pregnant and had ordered that lingerie. Everyone else was accustomed to Miles opening their mail. He tallied all of the things he hadn't prepared her for. With no other plan other than to try to get her to talk to him, he headed inside the house, not surprised to find her collapsed on the couch, crying.

He'd seated himself on the floor in front of her and tried feebly to wipe away her tears. Before he could even complete that task, a knock sounded on the front door. "Fucking hell, what now?" Wearily, he made his way to the door, recalling that Grant and Austin had also been privy to his wife's lingerie choices. If they said one word to her, he'd skin them alive, but it wasn't Grant and Austin at his door. It was Luke.

"Hey, man, Mom's on her way down here, but we got problems."

Rubbing his temples, Brock fought not to shout at Luke. "Can it wait?"

"I'm sorry, but it can't. Some of Gilbert's cattle is showing signs of ringworm. We gotta get them quarantined away from our calves and treated, and one of your bulls isn't liking life too much right now."

Brock's mind spun. Ring worm. Shit. What else was gonna blow up in his face? Untreated ring worm could be disastrous. Why weren't Gilbert's cattle immunized? The Camden herds were always immunized. The problem was there were a few of his calves that weren't old enough for shots yet. "What the hell's wrong with my bulls?" He rubbed his hands over his face. "Not ringworm?"

"No, not ringworm, but the one whose sac is making all the others jealous decided to lay down in the snow."

"Oh, fuck." Brock cringed.

"Yeah, so he's waiting on us to come get his frozen dick off the ground for him. He's probably not gonna be too friendly afterwards. I sure as hell wouldn't be."

Brock debated, but he really had no choice. He had a bull in pain, a bull he'd paid good money to get solely for what was in his sac, and it was currently frozen to the ground. Ringworm could be disastrous. He had a baby on the way. He had to provide for his family.

"I'll be there in just a sec." He assured Luke. Quickly, he set Hope's medicine on the coffee table with a glass of water. "I love you, darlin' so much. I'll be back quick, but I have to go take care of this."

She managed a slight nod before he headed back out into the snow.

Chapter Eleven

Crying until she was out of tears, Hope sat up and took the pills Brock left on the table.

How was she ever supposed to come back from the entire town seeing her lingerie? Surely, in this town everyone now knew that she was pregnant. What kind of mother would they think she was going to be? *Why did I even order that?* It had been in a moment of pure rebellion. She wanted to explore more, to learn more, to be with Brock more.

Like a child's flipbook, her mind offered her images of the things he'd taught her or allowed her to experience. She'd always felt alive in his arms. Now, he was never there, and she was tired of feeling like she had to fight for his attention. They were going to have a baby. She hated the very town his family founded. How was this ever going to work?

Before she laid back down, someone knocked on the front door. *What now?* Hesitantly, she opened it. Her brow furrowed. Aunt Jessie was giving her a sympathetic gaze while carrying a large stock pot. Holly and Natalie were right behind her.

"I know you've had a hell of a day, sweetie. Just let me get this on your oven." Jessie lifted the pot in her arms.

"You poor thing." Holly embraced Hope lightly. "I promise everything will work out."

"Wait? What? How did you know? *What* do you know?" She followed Holly and Jessie into the kitchen and refused to acknowledge Natalie. She was still irked with her on top of everything else.

Jessie and Holly shared a quick glance. "Well, some idiot put good ol' Mindy in charge of the Methodist Church's prayer phone chain. Word's always travelled fast around this town. Now it's moving at the speed of Mindy's mouth. I wanted to get to ya before the church called to set up a baptism date. A friend of Holly's was in Wilton's picking up diapers and saw what happened with Miles and your lingerie order. She was worried about you and gave Holly a call. Brock's got a mess of trouble with the Gilbert's cattle and that bull he bought yesterday, and I think it's high time we had a talk." Jessie winked at her.

Hope wondered what on earth had gone wrong with the cows now? She hadn't been able to hear whatever Luke had told Brock. Was ranch life always like this? Maybe she'd spoken too soon. Maybe she did want to go back to Gypsy Beach, to the sunshine, to a place with far fewer problems, to a place she already knew.

Holly shivered. "Why on earth don't you have gas logs?" She gestured towards the double-sided fireplace that shared a wall between the kitchen and living room. There was another one in Brock and Hope's bedroom. It was empty as well.

"Because your cousin is simultaneously the most stubborn and the sweetest outta all of you kids." Jessie rolled her eyes. "He won't use the money in the family accounts until he feels like he's added to it."

"Oh, good grief!" Holly huffed. "Men are completely ridiculous. This very thing will become reason number 758 why I will never marry a cowboy."

Jessie shot her the customary maternal look that said, 'shut it or I'll make you shut it.' "Since Hope has already married her a cowboy, and a darn good one at that, perhaps we could be more helpful, Holly Susanne Camden."

Hope's stomach turned. She hadn't eaten anything all day. The soup Jessie was heating up smelled wonderful and suddenly she was starving.

"Hungry?" There was a twinkle in Jessie's eyes that said she already knew the answer.

"Yes, ma'am. I'm starving actually. I'm getting a headache." That was probably due to the sheer number of tears she'd shed in the last hour, but food was likely to help somewhat.

"I had a feeling. Here." Jessie served a large bowl of homemade chicken noodle soup and set it on the table. She returned to the oven and began making several grilled cheese sandwiches. When the burner wouldn't light, she rolled her eyes. "I love that boy, but I'm gonna take a 2x4 to his backside."

"You have to use the burner the soup is on. It's the only one that works," Hope explained.

Jessie shook her head, moved the soup, lit the burner, placed the buttered sandwich on the skillet and then went to make coffee. When water began leaking out the bottom of the maker, several colorful curse words flew from her mouth. Hope found it cathartic to be laughing with Holly, but the soup was outstanding, so she returned to it quickly.

"Holly Susanne, come mind this sandwich while I go call your daddy. I'm taking over. Things in this house are about to change."

"You got it." Holly manned the stove while Aunt Jessie headed out into the snow with her cell phone.

Hope wasn't accustomed to anyone caring for her but Brock, and she was extremely curious to know what exactly had gotten to Jessie. She wished she could hear her talk on the phone. With a few restorative bites of soup, her mind settled. She tried to focus on the baby, but that was coupled with another round of her perceived ineptitude.

When her bowl was empty, Holly sweetly refilled it and supplied her the delicious sandwich. Unable to help herself, Hope dug in.

"Wanna talk about this crazy town, the baby, or the lingerie first?" Holly wrinkled her nose and offered Hope a grin. Natalie said nothing.

Deciding that she didn't care what Natalie thought, Hope spoke between bites of the delectable soup. "I don't know. I just don't feel like I know how to do anything here. Brock won't teach me, or he doesn't have time," she amended. "Now, we're having a baby, and I don't know how to do that either." She'd been fighting the tidal wave of emotions for too long to keep them to herself any longer. Brock wasn't there. She needed help. "This town is crazy."

Holly nodded her agreement as they heard Jessie shouting through the door and shared a curious glance.

A moment later, Jessie appeared, looking rather pleased with herself. "All right now, Everett's gonna talk to my sweet but stubborn-as-mud nephew, and I'm gonna talk with you."

"Thank you for coming by, and thank you for the soup. It's delicious. I'm pretty sure I'm just not cut out for ranch life. I'm weak." Hope shrugged.

Holly shook her head, and Jessie glared at Natalie. "Wonder where on earth she got that idea."

It appeared that Jessie knew precisely where Hope had struck upon the idea that she was weak. Jessie shook her head at Natalie. "I've a good mind to take a 2x4 to your little butt, too, Natalie Marie. Both of you listen to me. Not *one* of these crazy-ass cowboys or *cowgirls* in this town have ever done half of the things you've survived, Hope. You gathered yourself up and took care of your little sister after your parents were killed. You survived umpteen-hundred tropical storms and hurricanes back in that beach town. You opened your own business and kept it afloat. You showed my nephew what things in life really matter. You taught him how to love, and maybe more importantly than that, taught him that he is loveable. And when you figured out what his daddy and all of them coaches and principals had done, letting Brock's education slide so he could play ball, you marched yourself right on in there and told them all just what you thought of that. You're brave as hell, woman. Don't ever let me hear you say you aren't.

"On top of all that, you agreed to move out here to the middle of nowhere so Brock could have back what he lost when he was a kid. None of those things are weak. The way you love him, that's a strength most women can't even fathom. Things'll settle down. You'll see. Did I ever tell you the story of how I met Everett Camden?" A gleam lit Jessie's eyes, and her smile seemed to erase ten years from her age.

Grinning in spite of herself, Hope shook her head. Holly wrapped blankets around Hope's shoulders. Her mother nodded, and they each retrieved blankets for themselves.

Memories visibly painted themselves on the canvases of Jessie's kind brown eyes. "I was the top buyer in men's fashion for Dillard's Department stores out of Denver back in the day. I took over sales in the Midwest when I was only 23. Youngest buyer in Dillard's history. To tell you the truth, I'd never been outside of Denver, other than to take a few road-trips with my girlfriends to Vegas, but the stores in Lincoln and Omaha weren't turning over inventory, especially in the men's departments like they were in our other stores in the mid-west. If they didn't show a profit by the end of June that year, corporate was going to close one, or the other, or both. I was sent to see if I could figure out what men in this area were looking for so we could make better buys, offer better sales, and hopefully save the stores.

"Anyway." Jessie stood and made Hope a glass of water before continuing. "I left Omaha and headed west towards Lincoln, or at least that had been my plan. Only I got turned around three ways from Sunday out here on these country roads. It was way past dark. This was long before cell phones, and I didn't have a clue on this good Lord's earth where I was or how to get back to civilization. Like a dumbass, I kept driving. I drove until I ran smack out of gas on rural route 276. I saw no other option other than to sit on the side of the road and cry. I hadn't seen another car in well over an hour.

"Just as I'd worked myself up into a good fit, this gorgeous cowboy and two of his friends were tapping on my car window. I screamed, naturally, but eventually calmed down and got out of my car. I will never forget the worried look in Everett's eyes. Nobody in Denver, and certainly no one in Vegas had ever looked at me, concerned like that. My parents never did give much care as to whether I was all right or not. I took care of myself, and I liked it that way.

"Well, Ev explained that he could get me some gas, but that the stations wouldn't be open until morning, and if I wouldn't mind coming back with him to his family's ranch, that they'd be obliged to put me up for the night and get me a warm meal. I was terrified to climb up in that truck cab with three cowboys, but didn't have much choice. It was either that or freeze to death on the side of the road, so off I went.

"I met Everett's mama and daddy, and something kept Ev and me eyeballing one another while we ate. He took me out horseback riding. Even though it was darn brisk that evening, I don't remember feeling the cold. I just remember him.

"Anyway, I met his asinine brother, Mick. He wasn't any better then than he was when you knew him. He scared me, but I kept coming up with excuses to delay my trip to Lincoln, to spend more time with Ev. Told my boss I was studying up on what men in the area were wearing. Finally, at risk of losing my job, I made the trip to Lincoln, but I came back to the ranch that night at Ev's pleading. I just never wanted to leave, and I swunney the town ran their mouths 'til their tongues were blue about Ev and me shacking up at the ranch. People didn't do things like that back then. Finally, I quit that fancy job in Denver, but people in Pleasant Glen still didn't care for me. According to them, I was too uppity. It's always something. They like to try and pick you apart to see what you're made of. Eventually, they figured I was here to stay, and if they wanted to do business with Camden Ranch they might think about being nice, since Ev was taking over the family business." Jessie gave Hope a consolatory wink.

"Well, yeah, but I bet no one in town ever saw the really racy lingerie you stupidly ordered." Hope's face flooded with another round of heat.

Holly and Jessie both laughed. Natalie rolled her eyes.

"Hope, darlin' let me finish my story."

"Sorry," she apologized.

"Remember, I had a fancy department store job in the big city. See, Mick was always jealous of Ev. He was fit to be tied that Ev was marrying before he was. One day, I had a big shipment of lingerie samples sent up from the Denver store. I had in my mind I was gonna give Everett Camden a fashion show for his birthday then give him the night of his life. Well, Mick, signed for the packages. Naturally, Miles had opened the boxes, so Mick knew exactly what was in there. Ev and I had gone to Ogalla to pick out our rings. Meanwhile, outta pure spite that his brother was getting some and he wasn't, Mick took all of the boxes out to the cow pastures. You can imagine what my lingerie looked like by the time the cows got through stomping and chewing up the boxes. And dang it all if one of the steers didn't wind up with a black lacey pair of panties on his head that made him crazy. Covered one of his eyes. Cows don't like that. He ran through a fence with it. Cowboys were out chasing that steer in my undergarments three ranches over." Jessie shook her head at the memory. "I never thought I'd recover. There was even a picture of the cow with my panties on its head in the paper."

"Oh, my gosh!" Hope couldn't help but laugh.

"See, *now* it's funny, but when it's happening it doesn't feel so funny. Here's a little trick I've learned in my time on this planet — If you'll be able to laugh about it someday, try to go ahead and laugh about it now. It's not worth stewing, and fuming, and wasting life over it. People will talk about our idiot mailman and your lingerie for a little while then they'll move on to something else. There'll be somebody else to pick apart to see what they're made of. You'll see, Hope. There's a place on this ranch and in this town for you, sweetheart. We just have to find the right spot."

Smiling, Hope nodded her agreement.

"Something else I forgot to tell you about that lingerie." Jessie smirked. "Luke was born seven months after the night my lingerie made it into the paper. I was already pregnant, but I wasn't gonna let that stop me from living my life. Besides, I probably wouldn't have had five kids back to back if Ev didn't think I was some-kinda sexy when I was pregnant. I 'spect his nephew feels the same way about you."

"So, you think it's okay to wear lingerie like that even though I'm pregnant?" Hope was astonished.

"Honey, life out here on a cattle ranch will get mighty boring if we don't ever do anything fun. Hell yes, I think you should wear that lingerie for Brock. God knows he'll love it, and love is where babies come from, isn't it? Love's what makes this whole world go round and round. Love's the only thing worth having anyway.

"Don't let some preconceived notion of pregnancy keep you from being you, Hope. Women have been birthing babies since the dawn of time. Take everything with a grain of salt, and I am right here on this ranch day in and day out. Ask me questions. Let me help you. We're so thrilled you and Brock are here with us. We love you. We want you to be part of our family. That's the way we survive out here where the cows wear lingerie, the mailman's half-loon, and the sheriff's deputy took a squat in the cornfield and came up with more than he bargained for. This town may be crazy, but it's full of good people. I may not let Pearl and Sally come anywhere near my hair, but they'd do anything in the world for ya. Miles, too, as crazy as he is. We're all just trying to make a life out here in the middle of nowhere. We need each other. We get by together."

Suddenly, Hope found herself wanting a chance to become a part of this crazy town. It was full of good people. Lately, she'd focused on the not-so-nice ones, and that wasn't fair, either.

"Okay, now it's my turn," Holly jumped into the conversation. "I'm a psychology major, so I'm going to diagnose you."

"Just listen to her. It's good for her self-esteem," Jessie teased just to keep Hope laughing.

"I want to listen to her. I'm tired of feeling so lost. Thank you both for all of this."

"Oh, honey, we're not finished yet. I'm about to go out and make sure Ev's talkin' and Brock's listenin'," Jessie assured.

Holly rolled her eyes at her mother then turned her attention to Hope. "So, every time I've been home since you moved up here, you've seemed out of sorts and maybe even a little depressed. Mama would say you lost your sunshine." Holly winked at her mother, who nodded her agreement.

"It seems like you kind of gave up your whole life when you moved here, and for some reason you seem to think that's what you were supposed to do. You forgot to figure out what makes *you* smile, Hope. You and only you. You forgot to be yourself, and you forgot to take time to relocate your joy after you moved here. You need to find things you want to do. You're still thinking all your joy is back on the beach. This is an entirely different life, and I wonder if you're not still trying to live just the way you and Brock lived back on the beach. Maybe it's time to embrace the new. You might like it. You never know."

'Sometimes I feel like while we're in the car is the only time I get to see you smile lately.' Brock's words replayed in her

mind. "Yeah, I think you're right. You're pretty smart, you know that?" Hope offered Holly a grin.

"Well, I grew up listening to Mama give advice to every rancher's wife from here to Wyoming. I picked up a few things."

Jessie laughed. "All right, why don't you two head up to the farmhouse. It's too cold for her down here. I promise you, Hope, if Brock doesn't teach you to drive in all this snow, I will. But for now, you need to get warm and rest, and *we're* going out to check our numb-nutted bull." She jerked Natalie up out of her chair. "I have a few more things to say but they're all for my daughter here."

Natalie withered under her mother's glare.

"Okay, okay, I'm sorry I was rude to you yesterday. I shouldn't have been. I was annoyed that I kept having to drive you places, and my mouth gets the better of me. Brock and I were never that close, and now he's here running things. It irked me."

"It's okay, but I'm annoyed you keep having to drive me places, too, and Brock's not here to take over anything other than his part. We're family. You can be nice." Hope didn't have the energy to be angry at Natalie anymore. She was having a baby. It didn't even matter what Natalie said. Hope wasn't weak, but proving that to Natalie wasn't important. Proving it to herself was.

"Yes, you certainly can be nice," Jessie commanded.

"Wait?!" Hope gasped as realization settled in her mind. "Numb-nutted bull? Is that what you said?"

"Yeah, Brock paid hand over fist for a prize bull with a golden sac of semen at that sale from one of the only cowboys that'd agree to do business with him — all because cowboys can hold a grudge like nobody I've ever seen, and they all wanted to punish Brock for Mick's dealings. Anyway, damn bull got the brilliant idea of laying down in the snow, and his dick froze to the ground. As you can imagine, he's not a happy camper. I don't know who I felt sorrier for, Brock or the bull." Jessie and Natalie bundled up and headed out to check the herds.

Hope's mind whirled with all of the problems her husband had been facing entirely on his own. She hadn't been there to listen or to help because she'd been so caught up trying to recreate their life from Gypsy Beach. Brock wasn't the only one that hadn't been acting like they were a team.

"Come on. Let's go up to the house. We can watch movies and maybe go to Saddleback's for dinner if Brock and Daddy aren't finished working yet. Some friends of mine will be up there. I want to introduce you. Mama'll be back up at the house soon. Trust me, it doesn't take much to get her talking about birthing all of us. That'll help, and it's warm up there."

Taking inventory of herself, Hope knew she didn't want to be alone. It was freezing in their house again, and she still hadn't sorted through the shock of finding out she was pregnant. Knowing she could ask Jessie questions gave her peace like nothing else had. She wasn't sure she was up to dinner out, but somehow she did feel better. She downed another one of those wonderful red pills, bundled up, and climbed in Holly's truck.

Chapter Twelve

Exhaustion weighted Brock's entire body as he pressed a warm compress as far under the bull as he could manage. Austin tried to keep the bull calm while Ev and Luke worked with compresses on the other side. Suddenly, the bull bellowed and stood. Everyone backed up, watching the hot breath curl from his nostrils as he kicked with his right hind foot.

"Whoa there, you're okay now," Brock eased.

"Leave him be for a little while," Ev urged as they all backed carefully out of the pen.

"Hey Brock," Grant called as soon as they'd safely escaped.

"Yeah?" Brock still couldn't believe his day.

"Another tree came down on the other side of the big creek. Took out a huge section of fence. We gotta go fix it. I'm running out of places to keep the Gilbert's cattle away from ours."

Brock's head sank, and he fought not to whimper aloud.

"All right, you three go start getting Gilbert's cattle immunized." Ev directed Grant, Luke, and Austin. "Clearly, if they haven't had their shots, he needs our help. Then two of ya go pick up Grant's truck back in town. Maybe we'll all eat out at Saddlebacks. This day's beat all I've ever seen. Brock and I'll will fix the fence. We need to talk anyway."

Exerting more energy than he was certain he had at the moment, Brock furrowed his brow and then glanced back in the direction of the cottage. He'd had four hours of sleep in the last 30, and he had to get back to Hope.

"Your aunt's taking good care of her. You and I need to chat," Ev answered the unspoken question.

"Yeah, and you gotta wake up if you're gonna make use of the lingerie your wife ordered." Austin laughed as he headed towards his truck to drive to the back pastures.

"Fuck off, man. Why couldn't you just have let Miles leave it here? She'll probably never show her face anywhere ever again."

"Come on, you know we didn't send him back to town with it. He asked us if you or Hope were here. We said we thought you'd gone into town. He didn't reveal what he was delivering until after we'd said that. We tried to stop him. He was very insistent that Hope get it since it was *damaged.*" Austin couldn't quite contain his laughter.

Brock believed Grant had tried to stop him. He wasn't so sure Austin had helped, however. Grant had always been the peacemaker between all of his siblings. He tried to help Luke take care of everyone. They were the oldest brothers and shouldered their responsibilities well.

Luke shook his head. "Tell Hope people will forget about it soon enough. It's not the kind of scandal that people latch onto here. A newlywed bought lingerie. Who cares? How is that news?"

Brock prayed that was true. Convincing his wife that it really wasn't that big of a deal would be another thing entirely, however. It killed him that she'd tried to spread her developing sexual wings, and it had ended with an entire drugstore full of people laughing at her fifteen minutes after being told she was very unexpectedly expecting. If he were being completely truthful, it pissed him the fuck off that something meant to be shared between the two of them, something for his eyes only, had been seen by every person inside Wilton's Drug Store.

"Come on, son. We need to talk." Uncle Ev headed inside the barn. Brock begrudgingly followed. They loaded up fencing posts and heavy gauge wire in the back of Ev's pickup and headed towards the downed fence as the sun began its trek towards the western horizon.

Chapter Thirteen

The distinct feeling that he was about to be on the receiving end of one of his uncle's long, notorious lectures had Brock on edge. Couldn't anyone give him a break that day?

"You're a smart fellow, so there's a half-decent chance you already know some of what I'm about to say, but your aunt's gonna skin me alive if I don't get all of this out, and when a man goes on long enough being a stubborn dumbass, that automatically gives his kin license to say their piece."

Brock grunted his annoyance, but something inside of him told him to listen.

"Just because you spent the last decade building houses don't mean you know a damn thing about building a home, but since your sweet wife is gonna make me a great-uncle and since I *do* know a thing or two about raising up kids and building a home, why don't I talk and you listen."

"Fine. Go for it. I'm listening, but unless you have some way to make my wife like it here on the ranch, I'm not sure you can help me."

Ev rolled his eyes. "Funny how she don't like living inside a house that's cold enough for us to hang meat, with a stove that don't work, a TV that has no reception, boxes all over the damn place, other people's shit in the cabinets and drawers, and where she can't even have a decent cup of coffee. The fact that she let you get her pregnant is a testament to her kindness and patience and how much she clearly loves you. Your aunt would'a shot me twice, once when I was coming in and the next when I was running away."

"We don't have the money to fix up the cottage until I sell some cattle."

Ev rolled his eyes. "You own half of the largest ranch in this area, Brock Camden. You got enough cattle to make a pretty profit come selling time, enough to see you through several seasons and to put some in savings. We run this ranch together. There is plenty of money in those accounts to hire you some hands so you don't have to work your ass off constantly and to give you time and funding to fix up that house. You are currently working, son. I never intended for you to be slave labor. If I'd hired you instead of giving you your half, wouldn't you expect regular payment? 'Sides, you being damned and determined to do things your way and only your way reminds me of someone I don't much care for … your daddy."

If his uncle had backhanded him, it wouldn't have jolted him into realization any harder than that comment had. He'd been so determined to prove that he wasn't his old man he was acting just like him.

"So far today, Hope's been on the receiving end of a hefty dose of humiliation at the hands of our deputy sheriff, Mindy the loudmouth, and our mailman. She and the entire rest of the town found out she was pregnant. Don't seem to me like that was something you were expecting, so I kind of doubt she was either. I was standing at your door last night when we came to get you for the fire. I saw how terrified she was. You stuck her up in that freezing cold house and went to work, son. Don't take a genius to figure out that she's lost, scared, and frustrated. On top of all of that, she's pregnant. I left all the betting to your daddy, but I think it'd be a safe wager to say suddenly figuring out that you gotta grow a baby healthy inside of ya and then raise it up once it's outside of ya is scary as hell. Now, *I* know how hard this life is, and *you* know how hard this life is, but did it ever occur to you that you might need to help *her* understand this life and how hard it is?

103

"Killing yourself trying to do the work of ten men so you make more profit ain't getting the message across to her that you love her and cherish her. You're making money, but money ain't what she's needing. I suspect she'd far rather have her husband in her arms than a pile of cash in the bank. You need to learn that now, son. You're still letting the fear of losing this ranch drive you. This ranch is yours. You are not your daddy, Brock. You're not gonna gamble it away, and I'll tell you something else. No amount of money sitting in that bank is gonna matter if you lose your wife earning it. Marriage ain't the easiest thing in this world. It takes a whole lot of work. You both have to learn to build a life together. It takes a little finesse and a whole lotta time. You'll get there, but you've got to get your priorities straight."

"Okay, I know I screwed up. I just don't know what to do now."

The rhythmic click of the parking brake alerted Brock to the downed fence ahead of them. He followed Ev out of the truck and set to work clearing the snow so they could tamp new posts.

"You wanna know how to fix this, listen up," Ev huffed. "You think about her and what might make her life a little easier. You remember that she's gonna bring your child into this world, and that's a gift no one else can give you. You remember that she's scared. You tell her constantly how beautiful and how smart she is because the world don't seem to have figured out how miraculous women are. Most men don't ever want to see how strong they are, or how much they accomplish. 'Spose their dicks get cramped when they begin to understand that we are woefully lost without them."

"She is beautiful. She's amazing," Brock vowed adamantly. "I don't ever want to do anything without her. I know how much stronger she is than me."

"Don't tell me. Tell her. Tell her you're gonna be there when the baby's up all night sick and crying. Tell her you're gonna be there to hold her hand while she gives birth, and that you know she didn't get pregnant on her own. Tell her you're gonna change diapers, and give bottles, and teach 'um to ride, and to help Hope with anything that comes up. Diaper rash, colic, homework, broken arms, braces, gettin' thrown, tell her that you're in this for the long haul. Endless amounts of snow, bulls, babies, illness, calls from the schools, wrinkles, all the tears, and all the laughter, for the weight she's gonna insist she needs to lose that you know she doesn't, ovens that won't work, coffee makers that don't make coffee, crazy-ass mailmen, busybodies that want to tell her how to exist, house repairs … life. Make sure she knows that you have no intention of leaving her in a cold house to deal with *life* alone, because so far that's about all you've shown her you're gonna do. And, son, if there's something the two of you just can't figure out, I am right here, and I'm not going anywhere. I do have a little experience with ranching and raising up youngins."

Chapter Fourteen

"So, you're sure it's okay to have coffee?" Hope continued to pelt Aunt Jessie with question after question about pregnancy.

Jessie gave her a sweet grin. "Well, here's how I figure it. We're rancher's wives. Our husbands get up at the ass-crack of dawn. It's kinda nice if we get up with them. I, however, am not capable of getting up and even locating my kitchen, much less Ev's truck without a cup of coffee or two. The baby will be fine, just don't overdo it."

Hope considered each part of Jessie's advice. She'd never gotten up with Brock. She hadn't even thought to. It would be nice to be with him in the mornings. She kept expecting him to teach her about the ranch, but that was hard to do when she was never out with him on their expansive property. Jessie's matter-of-fact approach to life and children further restored Hope. Glancing out the windows on the kitchen door, she wondered when Brock might be back. They needed to talk. She had a lot to apologize for. He was out there in the freezing cold wind, trying to save their bull and repair yet another fence Jessie told her had come down. The regret ate at her.

"Holly, would you mind driving me out to wherever Brock is working. I just … kind of want to see him." Hope implored.

Jessie beamed at Hope. "They're down on the south pasture near Grant's land. You two go check up on 'um then head on to Saddlebacks and get us some tables. It's getting to be dinner time. We'll meet you there."

Hope wasn't anxious to leave the blazing fire in the warm farmhouse living room, but it was high time she took responsibility for her part of their current life, the one she'd been certain she couldn't stand a few hours before, the one she'd never really given a chance.

Reminding herself that Jessie had ridden along the same bumping paths while she was pregnant and that all five of her kids were perfectly healthy, Hope told herself that the baby was fine and focused on what to say to her husband.

His head lifted when the roar of the truck motor reached his ears. She watched panic flash in his eyes. He drove one more nail through the metal fencing into the post then headed her way.

"You okay, sugar? What are you doing out here?"

"I'm okay. I feel much better, really. I wanted to see you." She threw her arms around him. "I'm so sorry for everything I said in the doctor's office. I was just scared and being selfish. I don't hate it here."

Hope watched Ev wrap one arm around Holly as he gave Brock a broad grin.

"We have a lot we need to talk about, darlin'. I stuck you out in that cold house and didn't teach you how to live here. This is all my fault."

"I guess I'm still not so good at not being afraid of everything." Admitting that out loud somehow brought her a sense of determination to control her unnecessary fears.

"Hey, life's been rough lately. I'm scared, too.

"You are?" Hope was astonished. He knew how to do everything there. What on earth was he afraid of?

"Scared as hell, but we're gonna get through this together. I'm gonna be there for every single thing. I promise you. Let me finish up this fence and then we'll go get some dinner, okay? We can talk all night if we need to."

"Aunt Jessie told us to go on to Saddlebacks."

"Yeah, I don't want you out in this wind. I'll meet you there as soon as I get a shower."

"Hope, these are my girls, Lucy Keller, Cheyenne Miller, and McKayla Harris." Holly made introductions an hour later as they joined the ladies in the large corner booth in Saddlebacks. Holly told the bartender that her entire family would be in to eat soon.

"It's nice to meet you." Hope wondered when she would finally know everyone in town. They settled in. The other women had ordered platters of appetizers for their table. Hope stared longingly at the chips and dip, one of her favorites. Something she hadn't thought to buy lately. *You can't eat other people's food, Hope.*

"Go ahead, honey. When I was pregnant with Jamie, I was starving all the time. I almost stabbed James' hand with a fork when he tried to eat some spinach dip I wanted." Lucy laughed.

"Lucy married James Keller last year. He's over there playing darts. And this is baby Jamie." Holly pointed to a tiny, sleeping infant in a car seat beside Lucy.

"He's adorable," Hope swooned. "How old is he?"

"Four months." Lucy beamed down at her sleeping son. "You have any questions, you just give me a call."

"Thanks." Hope didn't really know these women, but somehow she felt accepted.

"You can call any of us and ask us anything, but me, McKayla, and Cheyenne have a pact. We're not marrying anyone from this town," Holly vowed. "So, we might not be too much help in that department."

"Or any surrounding town as they're full of cowboys, too," McKayla added vehemently.

"I never agreed to that." Cheyenne blushed and gave Hope a very kind grin. "It just has to be the *right* cowboy."

"Cheyenne's had a thing for my big brother for years. He's too stupid to notice," Holly chided.

"Which one?" Hope couldn't help but smile. Despite the freezing cold temperatures, a sudden warmth melted through a little more of the anguish she'd been carrying like a badge of honor lately.

"Grant, but please don't tell him," Cheyenne pled.

Hope loved the way she pronounced Grant's name, slow and Southern with an elongated a. Cheyenne was not from Nebraska that was certain.

"Hope would never do that." Holly vowed. Her word seemed to be good enough for the other ladies.

"I wouldn't. I swear. Where are you from?"

"Ever heard of a little town called Electra, Texas? My family moved up here when I was in middle school. I fought hard to hang on to my accent." She winked at Hope.

Hope nodded her understanding. "I had a crush on Brock for years, but I was terrified to tell him."

"Really? How'd you finally work up the courage?"

"Honestly, my friends kind of pushed me into it."

"Ooh!" Holly's eyes sparkled in the moonlight streaming through the windows. "We should do that for you. How about if you don't tell my big brother, who I'm telling you is gross, that you want him to bang your brains out, then I'll tell him." She cracked up, but Cheyenne's mouth hung open in horror.

"You will do no such thing! I'll run you over with my car, girl, and don't think I won't."

The entire table erupted in laughter.

"And Grant is not gross." Cheyenne added as she pulled the cherry out of her drink and popped it into her mouth when they simmered down.

Holly rolled her eyes. "Grant is gross. Not as gross as Austin, but almost. I grew up with them. I couldn't even saddle my horse without finding Playboys hidden most everywhere in the barn. I walked in on Grant and Heidi Carlson back when they were in college. He was … ugh .. instructing her in our barn!" An involuntary shudder worked through Holly as she gagged. "That's why I went into psychology, so I can counsel myself over that."

Another round of laughter echoed around the table.

"Well, maybe I wouldn't mind a few barn instructions." Cheyenne raised her left eyebrow in challenge. She was a Southern spitfire, for sure. Hope wanted to hug her.

"Oh, my God, I'm gonna puke. Fine, go jump in Grant's bed, just please, spare me the details."

Lucy leaned closer to Hope. "Can I ask you something? I swear I'm not trying to embarrass you. I really want to know."

"Uh, I guess so." Something about the sincerity in Lucy's plea kept her calm.

"Where did you order that lingerie from that everyone is talking about? I'm dying to get something more exciting. I don't want the fact that we're parents now to make us boring. We want to spice things up, but that's not easy in this town."

"Even if she tells you, I wouldn't recommend having anything delivered here." Holly shook her head.

A warm flush pooled in Hope's cheeks, but she pressed on. "I ordered it from Hanky-Panky lingerie, but I definitely won't be doing that again."

"You learn to get around the occasional craziness this town offers up. They have a store in Lincoln. We'll take a girl's shopping trip one day," Lucy urged.

"Really?"

"Hell yeah, honey. You're one of us now. We won't let you down. If anyone messes with you, I'll back them over with my car, too." Cheyenne winked at her.

"And if there's anything you *do* want to order, have it sent to Hol's apartment near the college. She's our discreet deliverer," McKayla vowed as they all helped themselves to more food.

"I was going to offer you that, when you were ready to talk about the lingerie thing. I figured the pregnancy might take precedence over that whole deal. Oh, that reminds me McK, what the hell is the *Womanizer?*" Holly handed McKayla a discreet white box. She quickly stuffed it in her purse.

"Fancy, schmancy new BOB. Can't wait to try it out. BOB #1 up and died on me."

"BOB?" Hope's brow furrowed, and she couldn't seem to wipe the silly grin off of her face.

"Battery operated boyfriend," Cheyenne mouthed.

"Ah," Hope broke out in a fit of giggles that elicited a round of laughter from her new friends.

"Nothing changes. This was the background music of my entire childhood. What are you all giggling about?" Suddenly, Austin's low, graveled tenor broke through their laughter as he scrubbed his hand over Holly's head. He and Grant were standing at the table. After a brief pause, this brought on uproariously abashed laughter as the women considered what they'd just been discussing. Hope searched for Brock, but didn't see him anywhere.

"He'll be here soon, Miss Hope. We came early to get Grant's truck." Austin winked at her.

Cheyenne's olive skin didn't conceal the blood that pooled readily in her cheeks. She couldn't seem to take her eyes off of a slight patch of chest hair visible at the top of the button-down shirt stretched across Grant's impressive muscles.

Grinning, Hope glanced out the window and made a wish for her new friend on one of the many twinkling stars visible that cold clear night.

"Let's dance." Holly bound out of their booth and all but shoved Cheyenne into Grant's arms.

James left his dart game and offered his hand to Lucy, who was beaming at him. "Would you mind watching him?" She directed McKayla and Hope to little Jamie.

"Of course not. You go dance," Hope insisted.

"I am not dancing with my sister." Austin scowled at Holly.

"Uh, yes you are. You're going to dance me over that cute guy in a suit standing by the bar. He needs to meet me."

Seeing couples eager to dance, the bartender switched the music on the speaker system to slow, sexy Country songs.

Hope and McKayla shared a grin as Grant wrapped his arms around Cheyenne, just a little tighter.

"I bet she's in heaven right now," McKayla said.

"She sure looks like she is," Hope agreed.

"Do you think they have a chance?"

"I really don't know. I haven't gotten to know Grant that well." *I haven't gotten to know anyone that well.* Hope realized yet another one of her mistakes.

As the second verse began, a man with rugged good looks dressed in Wranglers, boots, and a flannel shirt approached their table. He asked McKayla to dance. She stared up at him with her mouth hanging open in shock. Hope nudged her shin under the table to get her to speak.

"Uh," McKayla shook her head and turned to Hope.

"Go on. I'm fine." Hope tried not to laugh at her outright. This guy was cowboy through and through, from his hat all the way to his spurs. McKayla let the man take her hand and spin her onto the dance floor.

"You, Mrs. Camden, are entirely too beautiful not to be out there on the dance floor." Suddenly, Brock seated himself next to her. Ev and Jessie joined them at the table, grinning.

Hope threw her arms around Brock and hugged him tightly, inhaling deeply of that musk that was all her husband. "No one asked me, and I'm babysitting. Kind of thought I should get some practice." They stared down at James and Lucy's son.

"Well, I'm glad no one asked you, because I'd hate to have to beat some sonuvabitch's ass into the ground for hitting on my wife." Brock winked at her as he adjusted the baby's blankets. Hope swooned as she watched his calm tenderness with Jamie. She couldn't seem to stop smiling that evening. It was a welcomed change from the despair she'd been feeling lately.

"All right, you two, I've been needing to hold a baby, so you go dance. I'll watch this little pumpkin." Jessie edged Brock out of her way so she could get to the baby.

"Come here to me, sugar." Brock stood and offered Hope his hand.

As they melted into each other on the dance floor of the only restaurant in town, he whispered in her ear. "I'm so sorry for everything you've been through, baby. So fucking sorry. I know I screwed up, but we have to fix all of this together. I need you to talk to me again, Hope. You used to tell me everything. I miss you like crazy. You're my wife now, and you've always been my best friend. Please, can we start over and do this right?"

"I want that, too, but there's so much we need to do differently. We can't work on this marriage if you're never home. I miss you all the time. We're never together. I know you have to work, but I want to go with you when I can."

"I'd love for you to go with me whenever you want, but I swear, darlin', I'm not gonna work so much anymore, just give me a chance to prove myself."

Hope stared into the pleading depths of his hazel eyes. "I'm so sorry. It's not just your fault. I didn't do anything but sit around feeling sorry for myself. I never tried to make a life here. I just expected you to make one for me, and that isn't fair."

He cradled her closer. "Wanna go on home and really talk this time? Even if it takes all night or all week. I want to talk until we run out of problems to solve. I want to talk about the baby, and the lingerie, and the house, anything at all that you've been feeling. I'm anxious to get started fixing this. I don't want to wait one more minute. God only knows what might blow up next."

"That sounds perfect, but I'm really hungry again," she confessed with a sheepish grin.

Brock's sexy chuckle made her heart skip its next beat. "I bet you are, sugar. I thought you'd already eaten. Come on, let's get some supper. I'm half-starved myself."

Chapter Fifteen

Brock grinned as a soft sigh escaped his wife. She was snuggled into his embrace on their sofa. He'd stopped in at Merle's before he'd met her at Saddlebacks to purchase dry firewood. He wasn't sure how he was going to keep a fire going until he could get some gas logs in Lincoln, but currently there was a fire blazing in their living room, and the entire house was warm.

After hearing all of her concerns, he'd begun his apologies by promising her that he had no intention of going anywhere, ever. He continued, "Not teaching you to drive here and not spending any money on us was ridiculous of me to even think, much less insist on. I work my ass off, and somehow didn't think we deserved any of the money. I was being stubborn. I can't promise I won't ever be stubborn again, but I swear I'll try to be better. And I will be here for every single thing, sugar. I'm so sorry I haven't been. Every doctor's appointment, every diaper change, every single thing." The warmth of the fire and of his wife's sweet grin eased the chill in his bones he'd been so convinced the day before he'd never rid himself of.

"I know you will, but I have to change some things, too. I have to be an active participant in our life. I've lived on a ranch for weeks and haven't even ridden a horse or been out with you to help you with all of the work. I don't know what to do about the library, or the house, or anything, but I want to learn. I should have asked you or your family instead of stuffing everything and trying to figure it out on my own. I think not knowing is part of what made me angry. I feel like I don't know anything, and I hate feeling that way. But I shouldn't have taken it out on you. I guess I just wasn't used to not knowing. I mean, I was a certified bookworm all through school. It made me feel stupid to not understand this town and the ranch."

"Okay, so we both have some things to work on, but I feel like I moved you up here and threw myself into ranching, trying to prove something to a bunch of dumbass cowboys that want me to pay for the sins of my father. In actuality I ended up acting just like him." He heard the disgust perforate his own tone. Shame churned in his gut.

"Brock, no you didn't."

"I did. I acted like a stubborn know-it-all. Just like him, I was a fool. I somehow made myself believe that if I made a lot of money right off that I'd shut them all up. People are always going to believe whatever the hell it is they want to believe, and the only person I ever want to prove myself to is you." He watched tears track down her sweet face and tried to wipe them away. "The reason you feel like you don't know anything is because you don't. I never got off that horse long enough to teach you anything. I dragged you up here, stuck you in a freezing cold house, and went to work. I don't know what the hell was wrong with me.

"I should have told you never to order anything in the mail that you don't want everyone to see. I should have explained how the ranch works and how the town functions. I should have taken you to Lincoln to let you buy things for our home, or new clothes, or anything that made you smile, even if I'm not around to get to see it. I should have made sure that you knew how to drive out here and how to get places. I should have warned you about people like Ms. Bellamy. I should have been here to answer your questions. I should have done a lot of things I just didn't do, and I am so, so sorry. Tomorrow, we're going to Lincoln to do all of that. As soon as I'm done with chores we're gonna figure out some way to make this house a home. I'll start the new addition as soon as the snow melts."

"New addition?"

"Sweetie, there's only one bedroom and one bathroom in this house, and they're small. I was kind of thinking our baby might need a nursery, and that we might not want to share a bathroom with our kids. Besides, I have to rip out all of the sheetrock and replace the old insulation to keep it warm. This house needs a lot of work. I'm sorry I couldn't get it fixed before I moved you in, and I'm sorry I've let you live in this freezing cold home as long as I have."

Hope glanced around her home. She loved the glow of the firelight but couldn't imagine how they were going to expand it. Brock was an amazing homebuilder, but that work was going to be even more work on top of everything else he already had to do. "That sounds like a lot of work. You're already so busy."

"I'm gonna hire some hands. Like I said, it was ridiculous of me not to. I can't do all of this on my own. I need to be here more. I'm sorry I haven't been."

Something else plagued Hope. Now that they were really talking and she was able to process things, her Gypsy sensitivities returned to her. "Brock, what you just said about acting like your dad, is that what scared you about the baby? Is that what you were talking about when I came to see you while you were working on the fence? Because you're not him. You're amazing, and sweet, and kind, and you do take care of me. We just kind of got a little off track."

He stared at her. The firelight flickered in his eyes. She watched his Adam's apple contract as he swallowed harshly. "Yeah, that's at least some of it." The admittance brought that all too familiar shame to his eyes. She'd seen it there for years. After their wedding, it had disappeared somewhat. She hated to see it return.

"Please don't think that. You're going to be such a great dad. I mean, I was really freaked out when we found out. I don't know anything about babies or being a mom, but I'm also really excited. I imagined it being a few years later, but I always kind of saw us having a family. I know it's stupid, and after everything that happened you probably never want to step on a ball field again, but I used to imagine you coaching little league with our kids." She felt blood pool in her cheeks as she laughed at her own fantasies.

Brock leaned and brushed a kiss on one of her overly pink cheeks. "I wouldn't say I never wanted to step on a ball field again. Football and baseball are kind of in my blood, even if I shouldn't have been allowed to play when I did. I just don't ever want our kids to play sports because they think they have to. I don't ever want to pressure them, like my dad did me. If they want to play, then I'll be right there, right beside you, cheering them on. If I can help them, I'll do that, too." He shrugged. "I just hope I'm able to help them with more than learning how to throw a ball."

Hope shifted so she could study him more closely. "What do you mean? You'll be able to teach them so many things — how to run a ranch, how to ride a horse, how to be an amazing husband, and you'll be showing them how to be an amazing father."

He shook his head and gave her his customary grunt that said he didn't agree.

"Brock, we both screwed up, but we're both willing to fix this. You are an amazing husband."

"I swear I'm trying to be. I'll get better. I just …."

"You just what?"

Gently he lifted her chin. A storm of panic crashed in his eyes. "If I ever do anything that scares you. If I'm ever too rough with you or with our kids, swear to me right now that you'll tell me immediately. If you want me to talk to someone about my dad, I will. I will never do to you what he did to me and my mom."

"Brock!" Hope shook her head. "You have never ever done anything like your father did, and you never will. Your father made horrible choices."

"So did I."

"Brock, please. You know you're not him. And yeah, maybe both of us haven't really been making the best decisions lately, but you know there's something you do that your father would never have done."

Doubt etched itself on every chiseled plane of her husband's face.

"You admit when you've screwed up. You try to fix it and to do what's right. You try so hard to take care of me, and I know you'll always take care of our babies. You love me. You love him." She caressed her hands over her still relatively flat stomach. "And maybe I'm wrong, but it just never seemed to me that your father knew how to really love anyone. He was really screwed up, Brock, but you've spent your entire adult life trying to run from his demons. Let *him* run from his demons. All you have to do is be here with me. Together we'll deal with our own demons, and we'll live our life."

"Him?" Emotion choked his questioning plea as he gently placed his right hand over hers on her midsection. His brow furrowed in confusion.

Hope beamed at him. "I don't know for sure, but I always kind of imagined us having boys … just like their daddy."

"God, I hope they're so much better than I am, but you're right. I've got to stop trying to slay demons that aren't mine to slaughter. And being right here with you living life is all I've ever wanted."

"There's something else bothering you. I can tell. I am part Gypsy you know." She smirked.

Chuckling, he brushed a stray strand of her long blonde hair behind her right ear. "Prettiest damn Gypsy there ever was."

"Tell me what else you're afraid of."

"Okay, I will, but when we're finished talking about this, you have to tell me everything else that's got my girl so terrified lately."

"I promise."

"I don't know. I just I want to be everything for you and the baby. I want to take care of you, and I haven't been doing that so well lately. And they're gonna need me to … and what if I can't … I don't know."

"What if you can't what?"

"Hope, most parents read to their kids. They read them bedtime stories and teach *them* to read. They help them with their homework. I'm not gonna be able to do any of that." He shook his head.

"Brock, that isn't true. You're reading so much better now."

"There are still certain prints I can't understand, and I didn't actually learn anything in school."

"Okay, well I'm just barely pregnant. I'll help you learn anything you want to learn. We can go back through all of the Davis lessons again if you want. We can go over anything you need help on whenever we're not working. We have a while before the baby will be reading, and we can read him bedtime stories together."

"Yeah, I'd like that. I want to learn whatever they need me to know."

"Believe me, I do understand that. I have no idea what to do about anything. I don't know how to have a baby or feed a baby. The last diaper I helped change was my little sister's, and I was only four."

"Well, why don't we learn all of that stuff together, too? I've bottle fed calves. Can't be that different, right?" Brock winked at her.

Giggling, she shook her head at him and rolled her eyes.

"I love you, Hope, so much."

"I love you, too. So, we still have a lot to talk about, huh?"

"Yeah, and we're not stopping until we get through it all. Can we talk about the library first, sugar? Let's take everything one at a time. I've needed to talk to you about this for a while, and I just haven't."

A sense of loss welled in Hope's chest. "Do you want me to quit?"

"No, God no, that's not it. I don't want you to quit. I know you love your work, but …"

Shocked at his vehemence that she not quit, Hope wondered how she was going to keep working once the baby arrived. "But …?"

"When I lived here before, the library was open Wednesdays and Saturdays. According to Uncle Ev, at some point, the town changed it to Tuesdays and Saturdays because the church basement flooded, and the Lady's Aide Society wanted to use the library for their Wednesday meetings until repairs could be made.

"It's a little tough on the trucks getting you to and from work every single day. We really don't live close enough to town to make a trip like that six days a week, and your salary isn't enough to cover the wear and tear on the trucks. If you want to keep it open six days a week, I will figure out a way to make it work. I promise you. But if you want to learn more about the ranch, maybe hang out with me, and help out a little, and that would all be easier if you weren't at work so much. I'd love to have you with me more. I'd love to have you with me all the time. On a normal week, if we ever get one of those, I'll be here in the afternoons, when the morning work is done. Sometimes I have to go check everything at night, but you're never here in the afternoons when we could hang out and talk. I'm sure Aunt Jessie will be happy to watch the baby whenever you need to be at the library, and I'll take them out with me once they're old enough for that. I'll stay home with them when I can. I guess I was just wondering if I made our home a place you actually wanted to be, if you'd mind only opening the library a few days a week?"

"I'm guessing my salary also wouldn't be enough to pay the hands to work so you can stay home."

"It'll help with that some, but not to pay them full-time. Six days a week would actually be overtime."

"I don't want to work so much anymore. I want to be here with you. I went to work to escape being here. I somehow felt a little less inept there. I know how a library works, after all. There really aren't enough customers in this town to justify me working every day anyway. I knew that. I just didn't want to admit it. Two days a week and being with you all the other days sounds really good to me. Promise that's what will happen, and that we'll somehow make this house warmer," she negotiated.

"I swear to you, darlin', we're going to Lincoln tomorrow right after chores to get gas logs and the insulation. New stove, new HVAC unit, and anything else we need. And a new coffee maker. You know, so you can shoot the old one." He winked at her as Hope doubled over laughing.

"Okay so I went a little insane yesterday, but I had a really bad day."

Brock joined her laughted. She loved the way their laughter sounded together. She always had. "Target practice would at least make it useful for something." He shook his head and went on, "And it did occur to me that you might need some new clothes here in the next few months."

"Ugh, I've already gained so much weight." Hope felt guilty for lamenting the weight, but she was fairly certain the baby hadn't had anything to do with it yet.

"I think you're the most beautiful thing I've ever seen. You've gained weight where you always should have had it. You're actually eating now, and damn, baby, but those curves drive me wild. My God, have you not noticed how I can't keep my hands off of you? I'm pretty sure that's how you ended up pregnant. You've always been beautiful, but now … I don't know how to say it so you'll believe me, but you take my breath away. And this," he ran his hands over her stomach again, "I honestly can't wait until you're bigger. I can't wait to kiss your baby bump, come up with new ways to be with you when he's taking up your front half, and to see you swollen full of what we made together. I know we have a lot to change in the next nine months, but I can hardly wait. You're everything I've ever wanted, and you're having my baby. What could possibly be more beautiful than that, sugar?"

"Thank you for saying that. I just felt like everything I'd always known changed."

"And I wasn't there to reassure you," Brock completed her thought because he knew the part he'd played. It killed him, but he forced himself to learn, to remember the pain of this moment. As far as he could tell, marriage was made up of millions and millions of moments. He wanted so badly for all of hers to be good, but that wasn't the way life worked. He needed to remember this moment so he never repeated his mistakes.

Hope nuzzled her head on his shoulder. He was pretty sure she'd done it so she could close her eyes for a minute. When another yawn overtook her, he was certain. He grinned down at her. "How about if I take my babies to bed? We can keep talking as soon as I get back from feeding and checking that fence tomorrow."

"I thought I got to go with you." Her sleepy voice reverberated right next to his heart.

"You really want to get up that early?"

"I think so, but I don't know."

Chuckling, Brock stood, scooped her off of the sofa, and laid her in their bed before he returned to put out the fire. Hopefully, the house would hold the heat in for the night.

When he returned she was seated on the bed, shedding her clothes. She pulled off the long-sleeved undershirt and sweater she'd been wearing. Her breasts were far too large for the bra making a valiant effort to keep them contained. Her flesh spilled over the white lacey undergarment. The rosy hue of her tightly puckered nipples made him salivate. A low hungry groan escaped his lungs. "Keep going, sugar."

Staring up at him, she popped the clasp of the bra and shimmied it down her arms. He took it from her and tossed it away.

"Is this okay? Is it okay to want you as badly as I do?" Confusion fractured her plea.

"I'm standing here gettin' harder than a damn railroad spike, admiring my gorgeous wife while she gets undressed. That's the way it's supposed to work, sugar. Now, keep going for me."

Her bottom lip slipped through her teeth. He knew they were walking a thin line. Sex wasn't always going to be the answer, but my God she was so damn tempting, he couldn't help himself. The warmth that had been absent from her for so long settled in her cheeks and darkened her nipples. She stared up at him in hopeful expectation.

"What do you want, darlin'? Tell me."

"You …" Her breaths began their customary pant that drove him wild. "But shouldn't we …?"

He halted her protest with a drawing kiss. His tongue explored her mouth, drinking in her taste, a heady cocktail of sweet seduction.

Her fingers trailed over his cock as it throbbed anxiously against its denim trappings. A timid moan quivered from her throat, igniting the air between them.

Breaking from the kiss, his mind was receiving just enough blood flow to debate how he should proceed. "Shouldn't we what, baby? I'll do anything you want."

Based on her next move, what she wanted was his cock. He raised his left eyebrow in intrigue just before his head fell back in ecstasy as she lowered his jeans and boxers enough to lap her sweet mouth at the head.

A groan reverberated from deep within him and air escaped in a low hiss between his teeth. His right hand tangled in her hair, guiding her. She gave one timid sucking lick then turned her head and sucked him harder. *You need to stop this. Don't keep making the same mistakes, Camden.* Using every ounce of fortitude in his chiseled musculature, he stepped back. As badly as he wanted to beg her to suck him off, to drain him of all of the tension and confusion that had come between them, he wasn't giving in this time, not yet, anyway.

Stripping, he crawled into bed beside her. His heart located a steady, contented cadence when she laid on his chest. "I want you so bad, honey. I can hardly think straight, but I kind of think you were about to say something along the lines of – 'shouldn't' we finish talking first.'"

She gave him a begrudged nod that made him chuckle.

"Trust me, I'll make it worth your wait, and when there's nothing between us, it will be so much better."

"Yeah, I know you're right. I think it's just …"

"Just what?" He cradled her head in the gentle strength of his hand and then ran his fingers through her long, blonde hair. Tears pricked her eyes. He forced himself to let her have them. "I'm right here, sugar. Please just talk to me."

"I think that when we have sex … it just makes me feel like you're here with me. Like I don't have to compete with the cows, or horses, or fences, or whatever else. I know that's selfish and stupid. I think I started relying on it. Having sex with you is something you only do with me." She shrugged and buried her face in his chest.

Brushing a kiss on top of her head, he hugged her tighter. "It's not stupid or selfish. It makes total sense to me, and I was using it for all the wrong reasons, too. I can't ever resist you, so I just went with it. I knew making you talk, making you confess that you didn't like it here, was going to hurt both of us. At the time, I didn't know how to fix it. But sex can't replace talking. We need to be able to talk before, after, hell, even during if you want. We have to make time for every part of this relationship, not just the physical one."

"Yeah, I really miss the talking part, and the longer we went without really talking, the easier it got to keep everything to myself. It was kind of like I got out of the habit of telling you everything. That's not how marriage is supposed to work."

"No, it isn't. Actually, I have a theory about all of this."

"What's your theory?" She gave him her sweet grin. It gently mended just a little of the damage they'd inflicted on their relationship.

"It's a little like we rushed to build this relationship, because for me it was like I finally had a chance at the life I always wanted. But maybe we can't rush to build this anymore than we can rush to build a house. We tried to construct a marriage without much of a foundation. We never really combined our lives, sweetheart. We spent a few months living in your rental back on the beach before we moved up here, but we pretty much just had sex constantly. When I wasn't banging you, I was trying to learn to read. We never figured out how to really live together. If I did something you didn't seem to like, or something confused me, I just threw you in the bed again and jumped on top of you. It was a hell of a honeymoon, but probably not really the best way to put together a life. Having incredible sex with you always makes sense to me, but sex isn't always the answer."

"Well, I certainly never complained."

Unable to help himself, he brushed his lips across her smile. It had been missing for far too long. "Well, I'm glad, Mrs. Camden, but we might've let the lust side of things take over the love side of things. We got a little out of balance."

"Yeah, but we both did it, not just you. I think sex is part of a healthy marriage, but you're right, we have to find a balance that works for our family." She placed her hand on her stomach, and Brock couldn't help himself. He eased the blankets back and dropped tender kisses in a line from between her breasts down to her bellybutton.

Her sweet grin delighted him as he worked his way back up her body. "What else do you want to talk about, darlin'?"

"We covered the house, and my work, and you promised to be here more. I want you to teach me to drive, and I want to go with you in the mornings some." She shrugged. "I think it will take us a while to figure out the pregnancy. I think we should try to take it one day at a time."

"Agreed."

"Other than the poodles and Kara Seeton invited us over to their house. She said you and her husband were in riding club together or something. And Carson Rupp said to tell you hello. I think that's it."

Brock chuckled to cover the momentary pain of the memory that played in his mind. "Want to hear a story about Pearl and Sally?"

Hope shifted to her side to stare up at him in intrigue. At one time he'd promised to tell her all of his stories. He was certain that would take a lifetime, and he was glad.

"Yes. I love your stories."

Smiling, Brock gently tucked a stray of her long silky hair behind her right ear. "I was maybe six or seven. Mick had come home late the night before drunk off his ass, as usual. I knew it would be bad when he woke up. I could always tell by the number of broken bottles on the front porch. Mama went to work early that morning. She knew, too.

"I got up early and tried to make some cereal without waking him, but I accidentally dropped the bowl. It shattered, and a second later I heard him coming. I took off for Ev and Jessie's, but he came after me. I made it their house before he caught up, and of course, Aunt Jessie gave him what-for and told him to get the hell home that she was taking me to school. I came out of school that afternoon and saw him waiting on me. He was still furious and had a whiskey bottle in his hand. He'd started drinking again as soon as Jessie sent him home.

"Luke fished a quarter out of his pocket. He and Austin called Uncle Ev at the payphone near the school. Grant went to get our teacher, but I turned tail and headed into town. I couldn't wait on Ev to get there to save me. Pearl and Sally saw me slink against the brick wall of the beauty shop trying to make it into the church. Dad was afraid of the preacher, so I hid out there when I could. Pearl saw Mick coming down the street. She came out and got me to come inside the beauty shop. Sally went to Saddleback's and got me a cheeseburger and more French fries than I'd ever seen. They gave me quarters out of their tip jars so I could get sodas out of that old Coke machine. I was terrified of what Mick might do if he found me in there eating, but I was also starved.

"They let me hide there all day and well into the evening, until they knew Mick was back at the bars. Sally went and got me a handful of those Matchbox cars from Wilton's, a cap gun, some crayons, and some coloring books. They told me I could come there anytime I wanted and stay as long as I needed to. They used to keep all the toys they had for me in a little shoe box under the record-player counter thing. Promised they'd never tell Mick where I was. I remember them saying that Mick wasn't man enough to come into a beauty shop, so I was safe there. Probably the only seven year old in the history of the world that felt manly because he hid out in a beauty shop after school."

Hope's tears carried Brock back to the present. "The point of that whole story is Pearl and Sally are a little crazy, but they're really sweet. Might've saved my life. I wish I could give you some kind of logical explanation for the poodles, but I got nothing, sugar, other than they really do want to give love to things that need to be loved."

"Brock, I'm so sorry," she whispered as she wrapped her arms around him and mended his battered heart with her love.

"Nothing to be sorry over, darlin'. I have you right here in my arms. That makes up for anything I ever had to endure." He brushed a kiss on her cheek.

"Now, I really want to let them do my hair and hug both of them."

Laughing, Brock nodded. "And Kara Bowden must've married Ken Seeton. I remember Ken shoving me out of a seat in first grade when I tried to sit by Kara." Their laughter dried Hope's tears as Brock shook his head at the memory. "As for Carson, dude's been an ass-kisser for as long as I've known him. I couldn't stand him when I was eight. He probably wants me to take out a loan he'll make a shit-ton of commission on. Next time you see him, flip him off for me."

Hope's laughter was cut off in the wake of a deep yawn. "We can talk more tomorrow, right?"

"Tomorrow, and the next day, and forever. This marriage is forever, Hope. It's all I've ever wanted. But we have to build forever together, every single day. But there is one more thing we need to discuss."

He watched his wife cringe. "I was hoping you'd forget about that."

"Are you kidding me? Thinking about you in that lingerie has been taking over my brain all damn day. How do you think I'm still going after only having four hours of sleep in the last two days?"

"See, you need to sleep. We can talk about later." She was far too quick in her attempt to bury her feelings again. He was going to have to put a stop to that.

"No, ma'am. Come on. It kills me that you wanted to explore and that it was taken from you, from us. Believe me, people will run their mouths about it for a while, but then they'll move on. I decided to just let them be jealous. I get to be married to someone as beautiful and sweet as you are that's willing to buy stuff like that to wear for me."

She rolled her eyes.

Irritation surged through his blood. "Listen to me, and listen good. You are stunningly gorgeous, Hope. Everything about you is beautiful, inside and out. You drive me wild. I know you feel my cock throbbing against you. That's what you do to me. God, you're my every fantasy, baby. How do you not understand this? I know you're embarrassed, and I hate that. If I'd had any idea you were planning on ordering lingerie, I would have stopped you, put you in the truck, taken you to Lincoln, and let you shop for as long as you want ... as long as I got to pick out a few things for you as well." He winked at her.

"I just thought it might be fun." Her cheeks glowed crimson now.

"Since I am the guy that I'm praying you bought that for, how about not being embarrassed with me, please?"

"But it *is* embarrassing. I don't know. I just missed all of that exploring we used to do back when we first started dating. There's still stuff I want to try out. But if I go with you to Lincoln for lingerie, I don't get to surprise you with it. You'd know I have it. If no one knew I'd ordered it, I was safe. Plus I'm pregnant now. I don't even know if wearing lingerie is allowed."

Furrowing his brow momentarily, understanding finally settled on Brock. "If you got ballsy enough to put it on for me, we could explore. If you didn't want to, you could stick it in a drawer and not think about it."

"Exactly."

"Why wouldn't you want to wear it for me, darlin'? And why on earth wouldn't you be able to wear lingerie while you're pregnant, other than the likelihood that it'll cause me to come in my shorts as soon as I see you?"

Another eye roll said she still didn't really believe him. "I don't know."

"Listen to me, Hope Hendrix Camden, you are my wife, and that makes me the luckiest guy on the planet. We just agreed that having sex is part of a healthy marriage, and believe me, having a healthy marriage is about the best thing we can do for our kids. You are gorgeous. I want you every second of every day. If you refuse to believe me, I guess I'll just have to show you."

"So you think it's okay for us to keep exploring and having lots of sex while I'm pregnant and once the baby gets here?"

"I'm gonna go ahead and assume you're not gonna want me jumping on you right after you deliver, and we'll take everything day by day like you said, but yes, unless the doctor says otherwise, I think having sex while you're pregnant is perfectly okay. We just can't use sex to keep us from talking."

"Okay, good, because I think being pregnant might be making me horny." She wrinkled her nose. The pink heat that had settled in her cheeks turned back into a crimson fire, giving credence to her concern.

Unable to help himself, Brock laughed. "So, how many kids do you want, sugar — ten, eleven, we could have one a year?" He winked at her and listened to the melody of her sweet giggles. "How about if I just promise to be here for anything you need for every day of this pregnancy and every day of your life."

"That sounds perfect."

"And the lingerie?"

"I'll wear it for you, just give me a little time to work up the courage."

"You know I would never push anything on you."

With that, she lifted her head from his chest. Her eyes held a timid hunger, one he recognized all too well. Fear staged an uprising with abandon in their emerald depths, so many questions. He'd answer every single one.

She wore nothing but the low lamplight in their room and a slight covering of sheets and blankets. *Perfection.* He was mesmerized by the need in her eyes. But this was different. He wouldn't allow it to be an act of concealment. There would be no more hiding. No, this would be discovery and affirmation. She needed so much more than lust-filled sex. She needed to be worshipped, adored, and set free. They needed to make love thoroughly. He sought to rectify everything that had gone wrong, to reassure her that nothing would come before her again.

"So beautiful." He cupped the globes of her breasts in the gentle strength of his hands. They were fevered and swollen. "They hurt don't they, darlin'?"

A timid nod and a decadent roll of her body was her only response.

"Need me to make it feel better?"

"God, yes," she panted.

"I'll be so gentle, sugar. Soft and gentle." Brock lowered his lips to the stiff peak of her right breast. He was starved for the taste of her. The hunger radiated throughout him, but he suckled gently, just as he promised. Her eyelids drifted closed. She trembled then melted against him. He had so much to make up for. Rectification was his only goal.

Hope's senses had been frantic every hour of this endless day. As Brock lifted his mouth from her right breast to draw on her left, they centered solidly on how good that felt. She'd been dizzy with emotion. Now,

132

against his steady strength, his gentle touch, his hungry sucks, she stilled. It was different this time. He took his time showing her his love. He sought the balance they needed. Her hips lifted against his, desperate to push the world away.

A low tortured moan escaped him. "I've got you, sugar. I'm right here. Just be with me. Let me love you."

With that, he pressed deep, hungry kisses against her stomach and settled between her legs. He used the ample width of his broad shoulders to hold her legs apart. Hope's body twisted with need. She needed him. Every cell in her body needed him to make love with her. She quaked as he gently traced his fingertips down her slit, driving her into a frenzy of wanton desire. All thoughts of her lingerie being displayed in a drugstore or of the freezing cold snow melted in the heat he drew from her pores.

Unable to help herself, the need far too strong, she thrust upwards towards his mouth, back and forth, desperate for him to begin.

"I'm trying to go slow, baby. You're not helping. You showing me what you need me to lick? I'm so hungry for that honey you make all for me." He tracked his tongue between her swollen lips then spun it around her clitoris in a move he knew she loved.

"Yes, more," she begged. She knew what he loved as well.

"You gonna fuck my tongue, sweetheart? Fuck it until I let you come?" His hands curled around her hips.

With no further provocation, he dipped his tongue deep, and she thrust hard against him. Her thighs tightened against the stubble of his slight beard. The friction abraded her inner-thighs. It juxtaposed with his soft tongue and drove her harder. The constant pressure of his bathing licks on her clitoris became almost unbearable. Euphoria sated her body. He was hers. He was there. He would always be there. This was for them.

Pure pleasure drove the worry from her. She gave herself over to the sensations and lost herself with a ragged cry of relief.

Brock brushed kisses along the most sensitive spots of her inner-thighs when the grip of her legs eased, and she fell back against the mattress with soft moans of relent.

"My God, you are so damn beautiful when you let me have you." He climbed up her body, covering her in his strength, blocking her from the world that had taken too much as of late. Protecting her, making her vulnerable only to him, the way it should always have been. "My sweet baby, look at me."

Her eyes fluttered open. Love lit the fire in their depths. "Are you ready?" With tender pressure, he slid his cock against the wet heat coating her pussy.

"Yes, please. I need you."

He reached and took her hands in his own. Pinning them to the mattress over her head, he entered her slowly, allowing only his head to tempt the tightening perfection of his wife.

"What do you feel, Hope?"

"You. More, please, I need more."

On a low growl, he entered her another inch. "Does that feel good, sweetheart? Can you feel how much I love you?"

"Yes," she gasped, so hungry for him.

"Mine," he breathed as he entered her slowly inch by inch filling every satin hollow. "I'm right here." He spoke on his first full thrust. "I'll always be right here, right beside you." Out and in again. Slicked with her dew. Her pussy milking and hungry. "Forever." Again, he pressed inside the silky folds of heat made for him alone. "You're all mine, forever." Her soft, replete moan answered his next advance. "That's it. Say it. Say you're mine, sugar."

"Yours," she gasped. "All yours." She obeyed as he pulled back.

He pressed in again, feeling her body tremble and quake against his girth. The sounds of her pussy lapping at his cock drove him insane with need. His muscles tensed.

"I love you, darlin'. God, you feel so fucking good." His low drawl seemed to further tighten the heavenly grip of her pussy, like a fist around him. He wasn't going to last. In and out. "You're so beautiful. You are everything to me." He chased his breath as she writhed.

"Oh, God." The pressure and the need made her voice low and breathy.

"I'm right here." Another achingly slow thrust, shallow and then deep with the next, in perfect rhythm with her need. "Right here with you. Look at me." Her eyes had closed again in the ecstasy he provided. He wanted to see the bliss and the love in them. He needed to know she understood what she meant to him. They blinked open, and he held her intense gaze with his own. "I love you. I have always loved you. I will always love you."

In and out again with constant, steady pressure, owning her. He baptized himself inside of her, drawing in the redemption she offered him.

Every intense suckle of her pussy against him throbbed through his veins and took up residence in his balls. Her body nursed away every single thing never meant to have come between them.

She tensed. His name hung on her lips. Streaks of heated passion painted her body in the most beautiful pink landscape he'd ever have the pleasure of viewing. Her cheeks glowed enticingly. Her lips were swollen and calling for him to set her free. He pressed in once more. "Just let it go for me. I've got you."

She bowed taut and came on his command. She quaked around him. A half second later, his entire body tensed as he thrust, filling her to completion, and bathed her walls with hot cum. It shot in heavy spurts, claiming her. She was his.

Withdrawing as gently as he was able, he fell to the mattress beside her and cradled her on his chest. Her deep yawn was coupled with a bliss-filled grin of satisfaction.

"See, sugar, we can even talk *while* we have sex."

"Thank you for that. It was amazing."

"I love you, Hope. Go to sleep, baby. I'm right here." Turning off the lamp, he brushed a kiss on the top of her head and fell asleep holding onto the only things that would ever matter.

Chapter Sixteen

Inhaling deeply, Brock let his eyes open a good half-hour before his internal cowboy alarm clock roused him for chores. He rubbed his hands over his stubble and blinked the sleep from his eyes. A warm, sweet scent filled his lungs, and a broad grin spread across his face.

Scrambling from the bed, he halted just long enough to locate boxers before he headed to the kitchen. "Are you really up, making me your blueberry pancakes? Because if I'm still asleep, I'm pretty sure I just had a wet dream involving you and blueberry pancakes."

Hope, dressed in another one of his sweatshirts, yoga pants, a scarf, and some adorable teal-colored fuzzy socks, dissolved in a fit of giggles.

"I *am* up in this freezing kitchen making you my blueberry pancakes. I haven't made them in so long. I had to use frozen blueberries though, so they won't quite be like the ones I made back at Gypsy Beach."

"They look and smell phenomenal, darlin'. Not sure what I did to deserve this, but thank you."

"I'm trying to find myself again. I miss cooking. After I screwed up dinner the other night, I kind of …" She shrugged.

"Gave up?" Wrapping his hands around her from behind, he cradled her back to his chest. While she flipped another round of pancakes, he caressed her midsection, still liking the idea that soon it would be swollen full of their child. "Sugar, you were sick. You are pregnant. I was being a dumbass. This oven is shit. You'd just fallen and gotten hurt. You've got to stop expecting so much of yourself. Give yourself some time. We're doing things differently now, but it's not all going to be fixed this moment."

"I know. I'm just glad we talked and that we're going to fix this. I'm excited to be working on our marriage together."

"Well, together is about the only way I want any part of this life, Hope."

Setting the spatula down, she spun in his arms, and he dipped his tongue into the soft, sweet, warmth of her mouth. She grinned against his lips.

"Nope, hang on. Keep kissing me. I got this." Laughing and kissing her at the same time, Brock managed to flip the pancakes again while keeping her cradled against his chest.

An hour later, with Hope tucked under a pile of quilts in the passenger seat of his truck, Brock pulled the lever to release the hay bales he'd loaded up that morning. The sun began its majestic ascent over the pastures, painting the azure blue sky in a thousand shades of gold, orange, purple, and crimson. In an ostentatious show of crystalline competition, the snow reflected its white opulence back at the sky.

"Brock, it's so beautiful here," she sighed as they took in the ranch scenery tucking them in its care.

"Worth getting up at 4:30 with me occasionally?"

Grinning, she slid closer to him and laid her head against his bicep as he slowly drove, scattering the hay as they moved. "Maybe more than occasionally. I like being out here with you."

"I love you being out here with me." He leaned and planted a kiss on the top of her head. "You still want a driving lesson tomorrow?"

"Definitely."

She turned back to watch the cows munching on the hay as they followed the truck. "Look, all the calves are hanging out together like a kids' table at Thanksgiving."

Brock nodded. "That's because all of their mamas are pushing them out of the way."

"That isn't nice." She stared down at their baby's current residence, making him chuckle.

"My God, you're adorable, did you know that? And no, it isn't nice, but cows aren't people, sugar. I swear we will never eat our kids' food, but things are different in the animal kingdom. The babes'll get enough, trust me, and the mamas are nursing, so they're hungry." He pulled the levers on the feed truck and released the cattle feed cubes, since grass wasn't going to be available for another month or two. The herds bellowed their approval, making her smile again.

"So, sometimes if there's a bad storm coming in or the temperature drops significantly, we feed them a higher density feed at night. It helps their bodies stay warm. But you have to be careful doing that too much, because when you feed them affects when they calve. We all need to be out here watching and making sure the calves are healthy and safe when they get here. We can see better and pay more attention during the day, so we prefer for them to calve in the daylight." Brock continued to try and teach her everything he knew about ranching.

"When you feed them affects the time they go into labor?"

He grinned at the fascination in her tone. She loved to learn. She always had. "Seems to. And I meant to tell you this last night, but if you ever encounter one near our house again, try to keep calm. They're really not that interested in you. Just stay out of what we call their flight zone. As long as the cow feels like she can escape, they'll leave you alone. Don't approach them head on. If it's a bull, you get the hell away from there and call me. If not, give them a wide berth and you'll be fine."

"Okay, I'll try not to panic again. I think I would have handled it better had I not just encountered poodles and Mrs. Bellamy."

Brock leaned down and planted a kiss on top of her head. "I'd handle Mrs. Bellamy the same way I told you to handle a bull," he teased. "She lowers her head and starts pawing the dirt, you get the hell away from her."

Hope giggled, but she shifted in the seat again and nuzzled her head against his arm. "You okay, darlin'?"

"Little bit queasy. Might've had a few too many blueberry pancakes."

Trying not to panic, Brock considered for a half second. "I've got some feed bags in the back of the truck. I can get one if you feel sick."

"I'm going to add *puking in feed bags* to the long list of things I never thought I would even consider until I moved to a ranch." She grinned at him, easing some of his concern. "I'm okay. I'm not going to throw up."

"You sure? I can see if Luke'll come run the truck for me so I can take you home." His eyes landed on a Sprite he'd taken out of the refrigerator before they left. Opening it quickly, he handed it to her. "See if that helps some."

"I was trying not to drink sodas," she fretted, but then downed a long sip.

The fizzy beverage did ease Hope's stomach. She settled in and let her eyes sweep over the horizon. The ranch was beautiful. She couldn't believe that she'd never gotten Brock to show her all of the property. It seemed to go on endlessly. It was a calm and comforting sanctuary from the rest of the world. Staring out at all of the snow-covered fields, she couldn't understand what she'd been so afraid of. The truck bounced and the feed trailers squeaked as they rumbled back towards the outbuildings where the feed trucks were stored.

Suddenly, Hope spied a large two-story home with a wrap around porch. "That's the last house we looked at back in the fall before I said I wanted to move into the cottage, right?"

"Mmm hmm, it is." Brock gave her a grin but concern still clouded his eyes. "That helping?" He gestured to the Sprite.

"Yes, thank you for bringing it. Um, it's the house with the big kitchen and all those bedrooms upstairs, right?"

"Yeah, sugar. The one that had all the paneling you didn't like. Why?"

"The one with the big fire place in the kitchen, and the one you said was really safe because you could see bad weather coming from either direction because of where it is on the ranch?"

"Uh, yeah, but I'm a little confused about where this conversation is going. I was trying to give you a feeding lesson." He winked at her.

Hope grinned, but her mind was spinning rapidly. With another quick rub of her hand over her stomach, she summoned courage and went on with her question, "Could we go look at that house again?"

"Sure, darlin', if you want. I need to put up the feed trucks, but then we can. Can I ask *why* … again?"

Certain she did sound a little crazy, she tried not to laugh at the confused expression on Brock's face. "I kind of wonder if we should move in there. I mean, we haven't even unpacked most of our boxes at the cottage, and it needs so much work."

"Hope, no. Come on, you loved that cottage back in the fall. You said you wanted to live there forever. I swear, darlin', I'll make it warm and fix it up."

"That's not why I'm saying this. I really want to see it again, please, before we go to Lincoln." She knew he wouldn't turn her down. The hopefulness he was trying to hide was evident in his eyes.

Forcing herself to look beyond the horrible brown paneled walls, Hope vacillated between certainty and doubt.

"Sugar, you didn't like it a few months ago. I don't understand why you like it now, if it's not because I did such a piss-poor job making a home for you in the cottage."

"You did no such thing." She seated herself on the cushion-less window bench in the master bedroom and stared out at the snow covered fields surrounding the house. Even with the brown walls, this house had so many windows it didn't seem dark. Dust danced in the sunlight streaming in the window. She grinned as she recalled her father telling her that good dreams traveled on sunbeams during the day and wiggled in her ear once she gone to sleep at night. As a little girl, that old Gypsy tale kept her scrubbing her ears thoroughly in the bathtub each night, because she was so afraid of nightmares.

Glancing around the large bedroom again, she drew a deep breath. It was time to put the bad dreams behind her. There were so many good dreams coming true right in front of her. "Don't you see, Brock?"

"Sorry, darlin', but all I see is my wife trying to make concessions for me not doing my job." He sank down on the bench beside her.

"Listen to me, please. Back in the fall when we decided to get married, I tried so hard to be brave, but I was still a little bit afraid. I knew we were supposed to move here. I could feel it, but I was terrified to leave Gypsy Beach and everything I'd ever known."

"I know, sweetheart." He drew her closer with his right arm and laced the fingers of her left hand through his.

"I was afraid to move, and the cottage reminded me of mama and daddy's old house. It felt familiar. That's why I was so certain I wanted to move there. But I have to stop trying to live in the past, Brock. Sometimes I think fear will always be my first reaction to everything new. That's how I've always been. I'm sure I'll always be cautious, but I can't keep making decisions for our family out of fear or frustration. I can't cling to what feels familiar because familiar doesn't mean better.

142

"This house has bedrooms for all of us without you having to rip out walls. It has a big kitchen and a place for double ovens. It has a garage for our cars so they won't have to be warmed up for so long before we can go anywhere. It has fireplaces everywhere, and it's safer. You said so yourself. We can see everything that might be heading our way. It's also closer to the barns and stables. You'd get home faster from chores. I'm going to have a baby, and I already have this phenomenal husband. It's time for me to really live in this town and on this ranch. My family is here. My job is in town. I guess I want to be a part of this crazy community. There's room for us to have friends over here. There's even room for your family to eat with us occasionally."

"Are you sure, sugar?" He didn't look convinced.

"We can take down all of this paneling, right?" She wrinkled her nose.

"We can either take it down or fill it in and paint. I can do whatever you need me to do."

"Some bookshelves down in that keeping room thing would be cool."

"Done, darlin', anything else?"

"Can we paint clouds on the ceiling of the nursery?"

"Of course, unless we do find out it is a boy, and then maybe we could paint Herbie Husker on there."

Laughing, Hope shook her head. "You are not painting the Cornhuskers mascot on our son's ceiling, Brock Camden."

"Kidding, I was kidding. I plan on getting supplies in Lincoln today. If you're ready to jump into ranch life with both boots, so to speak, then I'll be right there beside you the entire time, sugar. Tell me anything you want me to do to this place to make it a home for you and for our baby." He gently rubbed his hand over her belly again. The sensation made her heart stutter and then fly.

"That's it." She threw her arms around her husband. He embraced her readily. "I just want to fix it up *with* you.

I want to help when I can, as long as it's safe for the baby."

"You really want to move again?"

"We never really moved in the first time. We just sort of unloaded boxes and left them. There's still other people's stuff in our kitchen drawers."

"All right, then let's do this. Let me go count fireplaces so we can get gas logs. They had a new HVAC unit put in here just a few years back before my grandparents moved into town, and it has high-end spray insulation, so no heat loss. I'm gonna want to put on a new roof come spring."

"I'm pretty sure you can handle that." Hope brushed a kiss on his cheek. "Just please, don't fall."

"That will be my number one goal, sugar. Trust me."

"So this was your grandparents' house?"

"Yeah, several years ago. I used to spend the night here all the time. That front bedroom on the other side of the house can't be the nursery. The roof gable is right outside the window. Makes sneaking out entirely too easy."

Shaking her head at him, Hope couldn't quite wrap her head around having a child old enough to sneak out. She'd just barely managed to grasp the fact that they were having a baby. The kitchen door swung open just then. She liked the slight whoosh and squeak it gave.

"Sounds like we have company." Brock took her hand and guided her back down the stairs.

They located Ev and Jessie standing in the kitchen. Ev was measuring the hole in the cabinets where ovens were meant to go.

"She swears she wants to move in here." Brock shrugged.

"Well, if that's what little mama wants …" Ev winked at Hope.

"You're sure?" Brock asked yet again.

"Two schools of thought on arguing with a woman, son," Ev spoke before Hope could reply. "Neither one of 'um works, so start figuring out what furniture you need to get today. You're moving."

"Listen to your uncle. He knows what he's talking about," Jessie assured.

"You good with these floors?" Brock ignored his aunt and uncle's teasing and kept up his questions.

"I love the hardwoods. I just think hardwood floors with the paneling is entirely too much wood."

A goading smirk crossed her husband's face. He wrapped his arms around her, and, unable to resist, whispered, "I have plenty of wood for you, darlin'. Don't you worry."

Jessie and Ev both rolled their eyes, making Hope laugh at her husband outright.

Overwhelmed that afternoon, Hope tried to frugally pick out things for their new house. "Are you sure we can afford those?" She pointed to a large set of gas logs that Brock wanted to put in the kitchen fireplace. They worked with a remote control, for ease of use. Hope couldn't believe her husband's turn around on not spending money until he felt he'd earned it. He was following through on his promises, and she would do the same. She was going to make Pleasant Glen her home, although being in Lincoln that day was very nice. Disappearing into a crowd of people that had no idea who you were was rather appealing after the week they'd had.

"We're making a home, sugar. I want you to get what you want."

He'd already added a rather expensive coffee maker in their cart, and their new cooktop and ovens were waiting to be loaded into the trucks. She'd picked out new cookware. They'd moved some of their combined furnishings from Gypsy Beach. All of Brock's cousins had promised to help them load and unload furniture as soon as they had all of the paneling dealt with. Ev and Jessie had urged them to move the bed they'd been using from the cottage to their new home. They assured them that the cottage was really meant for guests to the ranch from spring through fall. It wasn't ever really meant to be lived in through a winter.

Jessie and Holly were anxious for Hope to finish all of the house selections so they could hit the mall for some clothes shopping. Another yawn overtook Hope. Brock grinned and cradled her in his arms so she could close her eyes against his chest for just a minute.

"You okay, sugar?"

"I don't understand how something the size of a pea can make me so tired."

"You wanna go on home? We can come back another time."

"No, we're here now. I want to get everything we need. I'll be fine."

That evening Hope got lost in discussions of their new home with Brock. A sense of contentment she'd been so desperate for had been with her since the night before. The space heaters he'd purchased that day in Lincoln made the cottage far warmer. They just had to remember not to trip over them when they returned to the kitchen for more of the cocoa Hope had prepared after they'd eaten supper with Ev, Jessie, and all of Brock's cousins.

"I got you a surprise today. I was going to wait until we officially moved, but I want to give it to you now," Brock confessed.

"Brock, we spent a small fortune on our new house today, bought space heaters for *this* house, and I got clothes I actually fit in. What do you mean you got me a surprise?"

"I wanted to get you this. I was gonna attempt to wrap it, but I suck at that anyway." He handed over a bag from Best Buy. He must've gone there while she was clothes shopping with Holly.

Furrowing her brow, she pulled the box out of the bag and gasped, "Brock! You got me a new e-reader!"

Grinning at her reaction, he brushed a kiss on her forehead. "You never read anymore. That scares me. There are two dozen boxes of books upstairs that you used to love that you never even wanted to unpack. I miss watching you read. I love how you get that far away look in your eye when you're off in some other world, and I like how you twirl your hair while you read and bite your lip if something gets intense. I know somewhere deep under all of that confusion I stupidly let you carry around, you miss it, too."

"I do. I miss it a lot. I don't know how I let myself get so lost when we got up here."

"Well, maybe this will help. This way you can download anything you want. You don't have to wait to go to the big bookstore in Lincoln, but I still promise we'll go out there more. And you don't have to order them and pray that Miles doesn't read them before you do."

"Thank you!" She hugged him fiercely. "I can download pregnancy books."

Chuckling, Brock nodded. "Anything you want. And I called Sal Cartwright. His boys are saving up for trucks and are anxious for some ranch work. They're gonna come work in the mornings before school some and then in the afternoons, so I can be here more. I'm gonna hire three more hands for the next few weeks so we can get the house done. Tomorrow, we'll get to work painting. I'll get the ovens installed, and you can start arranging things however you want them."

"Thank you for all of this, Brock. I am the luckiest girl on this planet, and I'm so sorry I couldn't see that for so long."

"Ranch life is tough, darlin'. Don't be too hard on yourself."

"Life is tough. Life on a ranch, life on a beach, life anywhere is going to have its ups and downs, but that doesn't mean I don't want to live it."

Chapter Seventeen

Hope white-knuckle gripped the steering wheel of Brock's truck as she listened to her husband's instructions.

"Okay, keep plenty of space between you and the car in front of you in case you come across a patch of ice and slide," he explained.

"Space. Got it."

"Relax, sugar. You'll be fine. You're not gonna hit anything out here." He gestured to the empty snow-covered pasture surrounding them.

"Except maybe a wayward cow."

"Nah, I pinned them up on the other side of the ranch, to keep them safe," he teased her.

Rolling her eyes, Hope drove in circles around the pasture. This was her third lesson with Brock. Jessie and Ev had each given her one as well. She was feeling more confident, but still wanted to be cautious. She was currently housing their child, after all.

"Okay, if you start to spin, turn into the spin and don't slam on the brakes. Just stop giving it gas."

Hope nodded.

After her lesson, she drove them to their new home. The walls were almost completed. The paneling was now painted white, giving the farmhouse a bright, cheery effect. She couldn't wait to serve dinners at the large pedestal kitchen table that had belonged to Brock's grandparents.

They were moving their furniture in the following day. She'd selected a few new lighting fixtures.

When she parked the truck, Brock headed inside to install the new lights.

Luke and Austin entered the kitchen a few minutes later. "You're in it for the women. Don't even deny that," Luke huffed.

"The women are a bonus. I'm in it because I love it. What do you care anyway?" Austin came right back.

Hope and Brock shared a discreet eye roll. It seemed two nights before, Luke had gotten irritated with Austin at Saddlebacks. As usual, the women were hanging all over Austin, and he was working his rodeo king status heavily. Normally, his brothers didn't seem to care, but when Austin had sweet talked Amber Swenson onto the dance floor, Luke had gotten furious.

"If you wanna bed Amber, why don't you call her up and take her out?"

Luke shook his head as he began handing Brock the pigtail harnesses he needed for the lighting in the downstairs bathroom.

"Amber's been through hell. Mitchell just up and left her one day, no explanation, no nothing. She's a friend of mine. I just don't want you using her and tossing her away, which is your M.O. Has nothing to do with me wanting her."

"Right." Austin rolled his eyes.

"Would you two shut it? You've been arguing about this for two days. Let it go," Brock commanded.

Mumbles of irritation answered his order, but Hope was pleased that they did stop fighting, for the most part.

Chapter Eighteen

Saturday morning, the seductive scent of his wife roused Brock. The sun was just beginning to awaken the ranch. Very pleased with the arrangement he'd worked with the Cartwright boys, he reveled in his ability to sleep in on Saturday mornings. Their new home was warm, and they were settling in. The evening before, he'd helped Hope unpack all of her old books and arrange them on the bookshelves he'd installed in the keeping room. That balance they'd needed no longer seemed so far out of reach. Swallowing down the terror he always felt when he thought of Hope driving herself and their tiny baby over ice and snow, he reminded himself that fear was no way to live life. Something he'd learned from his beautiful wife. He would take her to get her license that day, just like he'd promised.

He kept his eyes closed and allowed his hands to glide from Hope's shoulders downward, tracing the descent of her spine and then over the swells of her bare asscheeks. She was tucked beside him in a sexy little ball. Handy she wasn't wearing panties. My God he wanted her just like this. Warm, and sweet, natural, carrying his baby, and tucked safely in his arms. She was barely awake and trying to conceal a grin.

"I want you, Mrs. Camden."

"Do you?" she sighed.

"So bad, darlin'. I'm aching for you."

"I'm in one of your t-shirts, and I just woke up." Her confusion was evident in her sleepy tone.

"You're beautiful." She'd modeled the lingerie she'd ordered for him two nights before. It was stunning, but this, this was perfection. He wanted her satin skin in his hands with nothing in his way.

He savored her breathy moan. Her hand reached back and encountered his rock-hard cock as he rubbed himself against that sexy ass that drove him wild with need. He shuddered as she squeezed his shaft and then dragged her fingertips up over his head.

"That's what you need isn't it, darlin'?"

"Yes." The urgency in her breathy tone amped the hunger racking readily in his balls. His hands slipped up the t-shirt she'd worn to bed, now that they had a warm home. Her ample breasts spilled through his fingers as he grasped them, coaxing another moan from deep within her. He tried to remember to be gentle, but my God, he needed to own her thoroughly.

She sat up, allowing him to dispense with the shirt altogether. Tossing it away, he nuzzled his head to the outside curve of her right breast then brushed hungry, open mouthed kisses along the underswell. The flavor of her, the sweet tang of sweat between her luscious tits, the perfection of her, natural and open all for him, sent impatience surging through his veins. His muscles ached with need. Sucking and nipping at her nipples, his tongue swept over the tightened buds adding pressure constantly. He decided to indulge the lust side of things that morning. He was certain she wouldn't mind.

"Oh, God, more. Harder," she begged.

A savage growl escaped him, humming against her breasts as he bit and suckled at her in constant juxtaposition, driving her into a state of euphoria with his tongue. Her back arched as her body rolled, so anxious for more.

The pain and the perfection of it all had him slipping his fingers down her tensed abdomen to tempt her further into compliance.

Swollen and fevered to the touch, she was the embodiment of primal female, needy all for him. Losing all ability to be gentle, driven by his own intense greed, he speared his fingers deep within her silken channel to find her tissues drenched, just as he'd suspected. "You're so nice and wet for me, darlin'. God, such a good girl."

152

Her body writhed as he slipped his fingers almost all the way out and then plunged her depths again, over and over, until the sound of her slick dew against his fingers made him desperate to pull her over him and own her thoroughly. She tightened around him, squirming and begging in broken syllables of desire. "It's right there, isn't it, sugar? So close I can feel it coming. I know what you need." He indulged her clit with several sucking licks.

"Brock, now. Please."

In one quick move, he pulled his fingers away, guided her up on her knees, and slammed into her, burying himself in deep. His sac slapped against her ass, and she came on his first thrust. The epitome of his every fantasy, his every desire, and by some miracle his wife. He drove her hard, feeling her juices slick him with every savage thrust. Ecstasy sizzled in his veins. White pops of light clouded his vision. His mind singled in on nothing but her pleasure to push away the rapture his body craved. If he lost focus, he was going to come long before he was ready. "Take it for me, darlin'. Just like that. I want you to scream my name for me when I let you come again."

"Oh, God, yes." Her guttural tone shot another stream of bliss straight to his cock. She milked him. He throbbed constantly inside of her, feeling her press back against him as her body consumed his.

"Not yet, sweetness. I'm not finished with you yet." He groped her ass as he drove into her, squeezing and watching her supple flesh, pliant under his touch. The perfection of it all bordered on pain as it roiled in his balls. He slapped her ass, watching it quake and fever under his hand as she moaned her adamant approval and shook it for him. He squeezed his eyes shut momentarily, still fighting with himself. Shutting down his own release. She was all that mattered.

Reaching around her, he stroked from her opening, filled to overflowing with his thick cock, upward to her clit, back and forth, until she shook from need and collapsed against the mattress. She came hard, crying out his name.

Rearing up on his hands, he slammed into her once more. On his next gasped breath, he fused his mouth to her shoulder blade, leaving a marking of ownership as he gained his own potent climax.

When he finally regained his breath and withdrew, she was a quivering mass of euphoria, still shaking from the experience. Brock fought the regret that built in his gut as he stared at what would be a slight bruise on her shoulder very soon, and remembering that she was pregnant, and he'd taken her like a wild animal with absolutely no consideration of restraint.

Guiding her up onto his chest, the apologies formed readily on his tongue. "I'm sorry, darlin'. That was too much. I shouldn't have lost control like that."

Her eyes blinked open. She grinned at him. The pink heat that he'd infused her body with settled in her cheeks. "Um, that was completely amazing. I was dreaming about that just a few minutes ago."

"You're gonna have a hickey on your shoulder." He cringed.

"Yum," she giggled out the word. My God, how could she be so stunningly sex and so incredibly innocent in the same moment? "No one will be able to see it, right?" Her awareness seemed to be coming back to her slowly.

"Uh, not as long as you're wearing a shirt." He traced his fingertips over the darkening bruise beside her shoulder blade to give her an idea of the location. "So only me."

Leaning up on her right elbow, she stared down at him with her hair in a tangled mass from their passion and her lips drawn in a sex-kitten grin, kiss-swollen, the color of a ripened raspberry too long on the vine. He kissed her, gently this time, but still just as unable to help himself. "You're so damn beautiful. I just love you so much."

"I love you, too, and I've had hickeys before, you know?"

His smile faded rapidly. "Can't say that's what I wanted to talk about right after we had sex."

Laughing, she brushed a kiss on his left nipple. "When I was a little girl, I had this doll that had suction cup feet that would stick to windows. For some reason, I decided to suction cup it to my face a few times while my sister and I were playing. I had tiny, purple circles all over my cheeks and chin. Daddy thought it was hysterical. Mama didn't, since school pictures were that week."

Laughing with her, Brock wondered if he could ever possibly count all of the things he adored about his wife. He was quite certain numbers didn't go that high.

"So, maybe if we have a little girl we won't get her anything with suction cup feet. Hickeys on my daughter are going to really irritate me," he confessed as he considered the scenario.

"I hadn't even thought of that until you said I had one, so thank you for bringing back another memory from my childhood, and I'm glad you gave me a hickey because I think it's really sexy."

"Do you, now?" He kissed the sides of her smile.

"Yes, I do."

"Have to see what I can do about that. But you're okay, right? You're sure that wasn't too much?"

"I'm so much better than okay," she spoke through a contented yawn that made him grin.

"You ready to spend the whole day together?"

"Yes, but after breakfast, because I'm hungry."

Laughing, Brock pulled on some sweats and headed to the kitchen to scramble his wife some eggs. "When we get back from getting your license, I have you a surprise."

"Brock, what do you mean you have me a surprise? You just gave me an e-reader, and we have a whole new house."

"Technically this isn't only from me. The entire Camden family is in on this one."

Hope spent her day busy with people actually visiting the library, since it hadn't been opened in the last few days, and helping Brock when he struggled through a book he'd wanted to read as a teen.

After she locked up the library at closing time, she followed her husband into the sheriff's office. Their hands were laced together, which was all that was keeping hers from shaking. Nervous tension twisted up her spine. After all of her lessons, she was getting pretty good, no longer tensing frantically when the truck encountered ice.

They were greeted by a grunt of disdain from Clarke as he whisked by, purposefully bumping into Brock as he made his escape.

A smirk spread across Sherriff Wilheim's face. "Sorry, about that. He's still ticked about me dropping the tickets. This must be Hope. Nice to finally meet you. Gotta tell ya, darlin', the whole damn Camden family put up one hell of a fight on your behalf." He shook Brock's hand as they shared a laugh. "Apparently your husband didn't inform his family that I'd already dropped the charges that day he came in here and chewed my ass about it. Thought Natalie was gonna put Clarke in a headlock when she stomped in here and demanded that we tear up the tickets."

"Natalie came by?" Hope was astonished.

Brock offered her a wink. "Nat's a hard ass. Her mouth gets her into trouble, but she doesn't like anyone messing with her family."

"Hell yeah, she came by just before Ev and Jessie got here. I'm telling you, he'll probably never pull you over again. Holly came in and lectured us on the outdated psychology of traffic tickets, and something she called merit-based reward systems instead of punitive punishments, or something like that. I don't know what all she said, but she went on forever."

"I figured I'd let Clarke get what was coming to him," Brock huffed.

"Now, don't be too hard on Clarke. In his own weird way, he looks up to you. He always has."

"Well, I'm happy to be friendly with him, but he needs to leave my wife the hell alone."

"Understand that." The Sheriff turned to Hope. "We don't have all of the fancy DMV stuff like they do in the big cities. Just fill out this paperwork, and we'll get your new license made." He handed her a clipboard.

"Sure, no problem, and thank you for understanding about the tickets. I guess I was in a hurry trying to find the doctor that day."

Sheriff Wilheim held up both of his hands. "Have an ex-wife, have 2 daughters, and now have a girlfriend, I'll be the first one to vow that Clarke should have left you be as soon as you said you were sick. You promise not to turn around in the middle of the road anymore, to obey the speed limit in town, always carry insurance on you, and we'll forget any of it ever happened."

"Thank you, sir. I promise."

A half hour later, Brock and Hope waved to the Sheriff as they headed out into the bright sunny day. "The sun's out." Hope felt ecstatic. She didn't even care that Sheriff Wilheim had snapped her new license photo while she was licking her front teeth, as odd as it looked. She'd even added ten pounds to her weight when she'd filled out the paperwork. No woman told the truth about that, and eventually their baby wouldn't live inside her stomach, so she reasoned that deducting the other fifteen she'd put on was allowable.

Brock grabbed her hand, turned it over, and dropped his keys into her palm. "You're legal now, so you can be my escort." He cringed as soon as the words left his tongue. "God, that sounded bad." He shook his head while she laughed hysterically. "You drive, darlin. We're heading to the stables."

"Why are we going to the stables?"

"We have something we need to take care of."

Forty-five minutes later, Hope was rather proud of herself for expertly parking the truck near the horse stables, constructed out of old train cars that Brock's great-grandfather had purchased off the railroad and turned into housing for the ranch horses. According to Brock, most every ranch in the area used train cars to construct their barns, as well.

They hopped out of the truck and Holly appeared, guiding a beautiful, creamy white horse out of the barn. She was followed by all of her brothers and her sister, along with Uncle Ev and Aunt Jessie. They were all grinning at Hope.

All of the other ranch horses were darkly colored in shades varying from chestnut brown to black. Hope's brow furrowed. "Who's this?" Still a little bit afraid, she forced herself to gently pat the horse's long graceful neck.

"This is Gracie. When I was a little girl, I learned to ride on Gracie's mama, Ashe. She was the sweetest, gentlest horse around, but Gracie might be even better. Brock and I went to see Ashe and Gracie yesterday. We gave Ashe to the Wilcrofts for their little girl when I left for college, but we definitely think Gracie is perfect for you, Hope," Holly explained.

"You got me my own horse?" Shocked and a little concerned, Hope stared into Gracie's kind black eyes. Not certain exactly how to care for her own horse, she offered Gracie a timid grin.

"I thought Gracie could help me teach you all about the ranch, darlin'. She's as sweet as they come. Completely bomb-proof, but if you're worried about the baby, you don't have to ride her yet. I wanted to go ahead and get her for you. Holly gets all the credit for finding her, though. I couldn't have found you a better horse. I'll teach you to take care of her." Brock placed a few sugar cubes he'd gotten in Hope's hand and guided her hand to Gracie's mouth. Even the way she ate the sugar cubes was slow and graceful. Hope appreciated her tender care.

"I rode with all of mine until I was too big to mount them." Jessie patted Gracie's side. "You'll be all right, just take it easy."

"Come on. I'll teach you to saddle her." Brock took Gracie's reins, and Hope followed his instructions, trying to memorize the steps. She blanketed her new horse, then went through the process of saddling.

"I'm gonna need you to go over all of that again with me several times," she admitted.

Laughing, Brock brushed a kiss on her forehead. "As many times as you need. You know that."

"You're sure it's safe?"

"We're gonna ride right beside you. Slow and easy. We're not gonna gallop off into the sunset, but if you don't feel comfortable, you don't have to."

Refusing to give into the fear, and trying to remember everything Brock taught her about riding Izzy back in North Carolina, Hope threw her right leg over Gracie and seated herself in the saddle. When Brock climbed on Cinder, and Holly saddled Grant's horse, Aspen, they set off. Hope tried to communicate telepathically with Gracie to explain that she'd only done this a few times, and she was pregnant, and to please take it easy. Miraculously, Gracie seemed to understand. She cantered slow and steady, and Hope relaxed and enjoyed the ride.

Delighted, Brock watched his beautiful wife bond with her new horse. Her beaming grin made his entire year. He slowed Cinder to a trot when Uncle Ev's horse, Busco, thundered up beside him.

"Looks like your coincidental cowgirl there is finally settling in." Ev gestured his head to Hope and Gracie, who appeared to be having a conversation as they eased further into the pasture. Brock wondered what they were discussing. There wasn't an animal alive that had better conversation skills than a horse, in his opinion.

"Nothing coincidental about my cowgirl." Brock shook his head. "Whole lot of Gypsies got together and somehow God agreed to give her to me. Never know how I got so lucky."

Ev chuckled. "You know, I never put too much stock in that Gypsy heritage of your mama's, but if that's the truth, you tell God and all them Gypsies they did good work. She looks right at home. You tell them we'll take good care of her."

"I will." Brock hastened Cinder to catch up to his wife.

Chapter Nineteen

"Look there, darlin'." Brock grinned as he pointed to the pink blooms on the redbud trees near their home. He was thrilled to see spring was making a hesitant appearance. They hadn't gotten any snow in three weeks, and the ranch was finally showing signs of drying out.

She beamed at him. "You know, back in January I was afraid I'd never see Spring again."

Brock wrapped her up in his arms on their porch. He cradled her rounded midsection in his arms and a broad grin spread across his face. "Well, the redbuds mean Spring has officially arrived. Go put on a bikini for me." He planted a kiss on the top of her head.

"I think I'll wait until our little boy is no longer living inside of me before I put on a bikini."

"I guess I'll allow that." He feigned disappointment, making her laugh. "Have we settled on a name for our little guy or are we still debating?"

"I keep telling you I want to name him Brock Nathaniel after you, but call him Nathan."

"Maybe," Brock allowed.

Hope took another sweeping glance of the green fields surrounding their home as the sun set on the horizon. There wasn't a single cloud in the sky.

"I love it here so much. I love our life here."

Brock hugged her tighter. "Oh yeah?"

"Yeah. I have a great job. People no longer look at me like I arrived on an alien spaceship, nor do they discuss my lingerie purchases."

"Uh, no one's even thought about your lingerie since Nora Epperstein told the whole town that Mrs. Bellamy was moonlighting as a sex phone operator." Brock shook his head.

Hope giggled, but then continued, "I have friends. I have a beautiful house that's warm and perfect. I know how to get everywhere, and Gracie and I totally beat you and Natalie to the pond yesterday."

"I was not aware we were racing, sweetness."

"We were in my mind."

"I see." He patted her backside, caught up in a pair of maternity jeans she'd gotten the last time they went to Lincoln as he chuckled.

"I don't think I'm going to be riding her much more until our little guy gets here."

"We'll ride her for you. I'm pretty sure she'll understand."

"You know what else I have?"

"What's that, darlin'?"

"I also have a wonderful husband that loves me and always takes care of me."

"You definitely have that, and you always will."

Hope gasped and rubbed her hand over her midsection. "Did you feel that?" She was ecstatic. Every time their little boy made himself known, Brock's entire world settled.

"I think so. I can't quite feel him like you do yet."

"I can't wait for you to be able to feel him. Right now it feels kind of like butterflies in my belly."

Grinning, Brock spun her and leaned his mouth down near her growing bump. "Hey little man. We love you."

Brock stood, and he and Hope turned when Austin's truck rumbled down the muddy path near their home. They waved as he headed out.

"You think he'll be okay? He's been in a bad mood lately," Hope's concern pricked at Brock's heart.

"I don't really think he wants to try for another title. I think he's sick of it all. I think he'd like to give up the rodeo circuit altogether, but he's too damn stubborn to admit that to himself."

"Even all the girls that hang out around him because of it?"

"Yeah, even the bunnies seem to be getting to him. He needs to find the one woman that makes him want to settle down, but Lord help her, because he ain't gonna go down without a fight."

Before she could respond, Holly and Grant whisked up their front porch steps, arguing.

"Damn, Hol, I just asked how she was, not for you to pick out a ring for her. I'm sorry I said anything," Grant bellowed angrily.

"So, you just up and asked me how Cheyenne is doing but don't really care?" Holly retorted with a gotcha grin.

"Exactly." Grant was lying, and they all knew it. Brock ran his right hand over his mouth to hide his chuckle when his wife and Holly shared a conspiratorial smirk. Grant was in for it. He just wasn't aware of that yet.

"What about you? Who was the dude you were hanging all over at Lazlo's last time I was in Lincoln? He was twice your age." Grant reverted back to his ten-year-old self before Brock's very eyes.

"He was not. Shut up!" And Holly appeared to make the same time-travelling trip.

Shaking his head, Brock guided Hope back inside their cozy home. He closed the door on his cousins. They could go on arguing for all he cared. Some things never changed. Besides, he and his wife had some celebrating to do. He'd managed to figure out the first eight-months of marriage. He had a healthy baby boy on the way. He wasn't a total screw up, and he'd keep right on learning to be the best husband he could possibly be. As long as she was in his arms, that was all that mattered.

163

From the Author

Want even more Brock and Hope? You can download a deleted scene from Jillian's website.
http://jillianneal.com/content/bonus-chapters

If you would like to read the beginning of Brock and Hope's story, check out *Gypsy Hope*, book four of the *Gypsy Beach* series.

Coming April, 2016 – Austin Camden's story. Sign up for the mailing list to keep up with all the latest news on Camden Ranch.

Connect with Jillian

Visit my blog http://jillianneal.com to learn more about my writing, my family, and more.

Sign up for my newsletters and emails on my site.

Like my fan page on Facebook.
http://facebook.com/jilliannealauthor

Follow me on Twitter.
@jilliannealauth

Follow me on Pinterest.
http://pinterest.com/readjillianneal/

If you loved Conicidental Cowgirl, leave me a review on Amazon, Barnes and Noble, or Goodreads

About Jillian

Bestselling author, Jillian Neal, was not only born 30 but also came accessorized with loads of books and adorable handbags in which to carry them, at least that's what she tells people. After earning a degree in education, she discovered that her passion could never be housed inside a classroom. A vehement lover of love and having maintained a lifelong affair with the awe-inspiring power of words, she set to turn the romance industry on its head. Her overly-caffeinated, troupe-spinning muse is never happy with the standard formula story. She believes every book should be brimming with passion, loaded with hot sexy scenes, packed with a gut-punch of emotion, and have characters that leap off the page and right into your heart.

Her first series, The Gifted Realm, defines contemporary romance with a fantasy twist. Her Gypsy Beach series will leave you longing to visit the sultry shores of the tiny bohemian beach town, and her erotic romance series, Camden Ranch, will make you certain there is nothing better than a cowboy with some chaps and a plan. The sheer amount of coffee required to keep all of those characters dancing in her head would border on lethal, so she unleashes their engaging stories on page after page of spellbinding reads.

Jillian lives outside of Atlanta with her own sexy sweetheart, their teenage sons, and enough stiletto heels, cowgirl boots, and flip-flops to exist in any of the fictional worlds she brings to life.

For more information on the author and her stories, check out her website, at http://jillianneal.com